THE CONRAD POSSE

The Conrad Posse, the famous group that had set about cleaning up a territory infested by human predators, was disbanding. The names of the infamous pistolmen hunted down by the Posse were now mostly a roll-call of the dead, but the name of the much sought Frank Jago was not among them. That proved to be a fatal mistake for it was not long before Jago took to his old trail of robbery and murder. Violence bred violence, and soon death stalked the land.

Books by Frank Scarman
in the Linford Western Library:

BLACK CANYON
AN OUTLAW
SUNDAY OF THE PISTOLMEN

FRANK SCARMAN

THE CONRAD POSSE

Complete and Unabridged

LINFORD
Leicester

First published in Great Britain in 1997 by
Robert Hale Limited
London

First Linford Edition
published 1999
by arrangement with
Robert Hale Limited
London

The right of Frank Scarman to be identified
as the author of this work has been asserted
by him in accordance with the
Copyright, Designs and Patents Act, 1988

British Library CIP Data

Scarman, Frank
    The Conrad Posse.—Large print ed.—
Linford western library
    1. Western stories
    2. Large type books
    I. Title
    823.9'14 [F]

    ISBN 0–7089–5501–0

Published by
F. A. Thorpe (Publishing) Ltd.
Anstey, Leicestershire

Set by Words & Graphics Ltd.
Anstey, Leicestershire
Printed and bound in Great Britain by
T. J. International Ltd., Padstow, Cornwall

This book is printed on acid-free paper

1

The Shafto House Hotel, Daverne, 1879
In the long, brightly-lit room upstairs, treading the grey, blue-figured Brussels carpet, there must have been close to a hundred people, and now that the liquor had begun to loosen tongues, the earlier restrained hum of talk had swelled to a steady roar. Silk dresses of every hue were in evidence, frock coats and boiled white shirts, though some citizens were in salt-and-pepper tweeds, others in unaccustomed broadcloth, redolent of camphor. Otherwise the smells were of lilac water and cigars. Piano music had been playing but had now ceased.

Against both of the longer walls, plates of fancy snacks had been laid out on tables spread with white linen cloths. There were crisply-folded napkins, small china plates and polished silver forks, and many of the guests had now taken the opportunity to indulge themselves. Liveried waiters were gliding among the throng, bearing trays of foaming beer and shot-glasses of whiskey. Punch-bowls were at either end of the tables. Chairs of Continental design had been placed here and there for the comfort of the women, and there were several davenports.

Anybody who was anybody was here, being seen and seeing who else was here. The mood was bright and there was a great deal of laughter and ceaseless movement, an energy made of an amalgam of celebration and relief, the euphoria of release from something. Chiefly from fear.

Yet those of the company who were being fêted, though responding to each and all with courtesy, remained the persons of serious mien that they had long been known to be. Tall, darkly clad, black pants, black, knee-length coats, silver watch-chains looped across black, buttoned vests, blue shirts and black string ties; and all with hanging, dark moustaches. Unsmiling men. Edward Maidment, Samuel Corde, Dave Dryden and Bob Conrad. Four, only four, comprising what had come to be known and would pass into the memory of the territory, as the Conrad Posse. But now, on this mild evening in Daverne, receiving the accolades of the citizenry, this group had come together for the final time.

Dour, even unlikeable men, no doubt some were thinking, men who apparently were incapable of unbending, even in such an hour as this. There was more to it, though, than could meet the eye of the passing observer. Occasionally, Conrad himself, tall, looking out over the heads of many here, caught a glance from Corde or Dryden or Maidment, perhaps each of them, as he was, comparing this carefree, civilized scene with the brutal realities of their own back-trail.

It was a long way, for example, from the failed attempt to get Steve

3

Collier and Bradley Horning to give themselves up peaceably, which led to the highly dangerous, protracted shoot in the railroad yards at Travis, Collier finally shot to death while coming in at Ed Maidment with a Colt Peacemaker, a weapon of the sort that Maidment had encountered before, and Horning made a cripple for whatever life remained to him, while trying to nail Dave Dryden, and sorely underestimating that man.

Another world indeed, this gathering and this room, from the one in which they had finally closed in on Nate Tanner, the man without conscience, who had taken, at the very least, four lives, had robbed and raped, sometimes alone, sometimes with other scum at his back. Until they had got him cornered.

Conrad turned his head and had to ask her to repeat what she had just said. Emmie Naver, the slim, fair-haired Danish woman. His woman. Or so she was spoken of. Now her delft-blue eyes, having become bright from maybe

4

too many glasses of punch (though her low-pitched, slightly accented voice was controlled), were now slightly clouded.

'What's the matter with you, Bob? Why don't you move around, *talk* with some of these people? They're *here* because of you. A lot of them want to shake your hand. They want to be able to say you *spoke* to them.' He was unable to decide whether or not this carried a faint mockery.

Conrad's voice was equally low, equally controlled. To an onlooker he might have been complimenting the small, slim, delicate-looking woman on how attractive she looked. 'I'm damn' tired, Emmie. We all are. These people mean well, I know that. But this kind of thing is never easy for me.'

Between moving figures, seated on a davenport, and though her face was tilted down, Laura Maidment was studying them from under her long lashes. Presently, Conrad's face assumed again that familiar mask-like expression that could have meant anything but was in fact a reliving of the past.

* * *

The explosions made by the pistols were very loud in the confines of the building, and it was not long before the place, upstairs and down, reeked of gunsmoke and burnt powder.

His ears humming from the noise, Conrad went bounding from a side room into the empty, dusty lobby, to be ready for any of them who sought to come down the stairs; just so long as it did not turn out to be one of his own. The big, dark man with black moustaches had led his men into this town real fast, choosing an early hour of the morning, trying to catch Tanner and the three known to be with him, at a disadvantage. It had not quite worked out as he had hoped, one man very fly indeed, nipping out quickly, defeating even Conrad's efforts, shooting from a window, to nail him, a head-ducking, scuttling man clad only in a pair of shabby pants and soon vanishing among outbuildings.

As far as Conrad was aware there were no other people in the building, and this gave him a freer hand. Boots came pounding down the stairs and suddenly as a man appeared on the lower landing. Not Corde. Not Dryden. Not Maidment. Conrad and the bare-headed man on the landing opened fire together, and in the bursting gunsmoke Conrad saw his target punched around by the .44 lead, but shot again, deafeningly, and this time the man jack-knifed, his pistol clattering onto boards, and came rolling down the fourteen stairs to flop loosely onto the floor of the lobby, arms splayed wide.

Whoever he was, Conrad saw that he was not Tanner, but looked like a part-Indian. Upstairs, gunfire blasted again, and men could be heard yelling. Then, like turning off a tap, all sounds ceased. Seconds went by, a half-minute maybe, then Dave Dryden's voice called, 'Bob?'

Conrad called, 'Here!'

Dryden, a long pistol in hand but hanging by his side, came unhurriedly down the stairs as far as the lower landing. He said, 'Tanner an' one other,' and with one finger, made a throat-cutting motion.

'Anybody else hit?'

Dryden shook his head. 'Tanner only let go with a couple. From then on, it misfired.'

Now there was an irony, considering what misery the felon, Tanner, had wrought with pistols in his time, that in his own moment of direst need, such a weapon should sell him short.

'Drag 'em all out in the street,' Conrad said. In his black, townsman's suit and with his silver watch-chain looped across his buttoned vest, he could easily have been taken for a successful merchant.

So Tanner and the two who had been shot to death with him were dragged unceremoniously by their heels out of the crummy hotel and now lay in a sorry-looking row, attracting the interest of whirling flies.

Little by little, men and even a few soberly-bonneted women began arriving. No doubt there was curiosity over who these men were who had come charging in like demons from hell, their purpose, as it had turned out, to take Nate Tanner, and there were open mouths now when it was realized that the group was the one led by Bob Conrad. No direct questions were asked of Conrad. Tanner, now, however, was the subject of muttered comment. A man who had been widely feared, Tanner, dead, was a middle-sized, skinny man with a deeply-lined face and a receding chin, looking oddly nondescript and of no account.

While Conrad and his equally tall companions were standing in a group, talking in low voices, and the townsfolk were still staring down at Tanner, a photographer with a large, polished-wood camera on a tripod, an unlikely denizen of this benighted place, so Conrad thought, came along the boardwalk. Under the flash of his photography was recorded for posterity the sordid end that had come to Nate Tanner and two of his associates, whose names nobody seemed to know, all lying at the feet of four unsmiling, soberly-dressed men whose names indeed were known and were becoming, across a whole wide stretch of country, part of the fabric of legend.

For Tanner was by no means the first predator to fall to the pistols of these hard men. Indeed, over recent months, a succession of long-sought miscreants had been shot down or had been fetched back to a waiting rope. All this carried out by four men whose principal was Robert Raines Conrad, an ex-deputy marshal, and three others, all of them once-lawmen and hand-picked by him. What had become known as Conrad's Posse had come into being, and the fact that it consisted of only these four men had raised eyebrows at the time. There had been some questions over the term *posse*, for of course it was nothing of the kind. Word had been that Conrad's distaste for other appellations had had everything to do with it. Eyebrows had sure lifted when the results began to be seen. Those who had been responsible for shooting three people to death during a robbery at the bank and loan in Garvin, and others who had cleaned out an express car near Mayor Bluffs, with loss of life there, all fetched back across their own saddles or with manacles on their wrists. Rewards out for all these wrongdoers had been readily paid out by the bank and the railroad; and there had followed a succession of enterprises at the behest of other banks and insurance companies, cattle companies and mines, ranging across a lot of country. In some of the bigger towns Conrad and his men had come riding back to find enthusiastic crowds, among them merchants who depended heavily upon the maintenance of order. There was a general consensus that there was but one way to fight fire and that was with fire. Up to that time, the problem had been the seemingly impossible task of mounting a determined and sustained effort to get all these matters cleared up, which, of course, had to start with finding men of the moral fibre necessary to carry it through. Just who had been sufficiently inspired to put Conrad's name forward, then give him a free hand to select his party, was unclear, though there had been rumours that certain political influences had been at work, these propelled by parties with vested interests in this territory. As someone was heard to observe, '*A railroad can make more noise in a congressman's office than on a thousand mile of steel track.*'

None the less, there were tasks which were reckoned to be beyond even the Conrad Posse to resolve. One was the breaking up of a wild bunch said to be operating from across the border, that had been preying on cattle herds along the Menloe River country. Ranchers there, reaching as far as the Flinter Hills, had spent much time and effort and, on occasions, human life, trying to get to grips with the renegades who were driving off their beef. The problem might go away for a time, then resurface when least expected. Until Conrad, approaching, not across open rangeland but out of a narrow valley in the Flinters, hit a rustlers' drive during the half-hour before sundown, coming swiftly out of the blinding rays of the low sun, emptying four or five saddles with rifle fire before the rustlers knew what had hit them, turning the bawling, dusty herd back on them and killing three more men while they were about it. Among the dead had been a wanted ($15,000) piece of shit named Carlos Mendez, and with his demise, and the fetching in of his riven body to the cowtown of Menloe, there to be put on public display, the belief that Bob Conrad could achieve just about anything was given further currency. Which of course, doubters were still saying, might never extend to the apprehension of the Jagos.

2

As he knew she would do, sooner or later, Ruth Corde came easing through the crowd to where Conrad was now standing on his own, a barely-sipped shot-glass of whiskey in his hand. As soon as he caught sight of her dark green gown moving closer, he looked for a way out, but there was none, not at the moment, and soon she was in front of him, her glossy, pitch-black hair level with his throat, her green eyes looking up at him.

'Solemn Bob Conrad.'

'Where's Sam?'

She lifted a long-gloved hand in a vague gesture. 'He's around somewhere. Why concern yourself with Sam? I'd have thought you'd have seen enough of him to last you right through to Kingdom Come.'

Conrad was annoyed with himself

for showing his hand, revealing his discomfort, and there could be no doubt that she was aware of it. The slight, knowing smile on her full lips confirmed it. 'My my, Bob, and they say you never run from anything!' Now she really was mocking him.

'I don't know who would say that. Whoever it is, is lying.'

Ruth's voice, when next she spoke, was lower, and there could be no mistaking that her lighter mood had gone. 'Take the air with me, Bob. Walk me around the block. I'm near to choking in here.'

'I'll have them open more windows.'

'Bob, what's the matter with you?'

Precisely what Emmie had asked him not long ago. He knew that this answer would not sound convincing, either. 'It's been a bad time. Ask Sam.'

'There's not a lot of point in asking Sam.'

'That's no concern of mine.'

'Don't turn me away, Bob.'

'It will never be any good.'

'Walk me outside. I want to talk. I can't talk here.'

'No.' His hard face was expressionless, the slate eyes very still. Conrad thought, *there's no easy way to do this*. 'I've said, there's no point.'

'Bob, you can't mean that.'

'I mean it. It can never be.'

She could see — surely she must have known already — that there was to be no moving him, and the look that finally she bent upon him made even Conrad's eyes narrow slightly. It was something he ought to have marked well, right then, for he would come to remember it at a future time.

Lithgow, the Daverne mayor, with his feathery-white muttonchops, a glass in hand, came.

'So, Mr Conrad, this is it. The end of the trail. And a job magnificently done. I shall be having a word or two to say about that, later. Right now, as you can see, the folks merely wish to relax, enjoy meeting you and your . . . group, at close quarters.'

Now that we've been rendered safe, thought Conrad, somewhat sardonically. He said, 'We've been amply rewarded for our enterprises, Mayor Lithgow. No doubt there will be plenty who think excessively so, now that it's done.' Conrad thought about revising only the last part of that statement. *Not quite done*. They had failed to take Frank Jago. Gone to Mexico, Frank, so the word was. Conrad, however, let it stand.

'Those who might care to comment,' said Lithgow, 'from the safety of some saloon, somewhere, can do so if they wish. We can't stop that.' Lithgow's quick understanding of the realities surprised Conrad. The mayor then sighted someone else he wanted to speak to, and excused himself. Ruth Corde had gone. Conrad surveyed the chattering crowd. There was Sam Corde, talking with Ed and Laura Maidment. Laura caught Conrad's eye and smiled. A lovely woman, Laura, of calm, quiet demeanour, with golden-brown hair and large brown eyes and a heart-shaped face. She held Conrad's gaze for a moment or two, then looked away.

Emmie Naver, talking animatedly, was in a group of people only one of whom Conrad knew by sight. Dave Dryden had been surrounded, or so it appeared, by three women, and was as usual looking redly uncomfortable. The unattached posseman, Dryden, always made nervous by the close proximity of women. Right now he must be close to panic. Conrad smiled to himself and let his eyes move on. Gasely, the Daverne County Sheriff, small, round, tonsured like a monk, was holding forth, cigar in hand, waving it, making his points. From here and there bursts of laughter rose, glassware was clinking, the pianist, obscured from Conrad's view, had resumed. An executive of the South-Western Railroad, Poindexter, was here along with some wary-eyed men from several banks and insurance companies, conservatively dressed, these, drinking little. Seeing the bankers flicked Conrad's mind back to Audie Ringbold.

★ ★ ★

Fancy Dan, Audie. Thought a hell of a lot of himself. Dangerous, though, grievously so. As it happened, Conrad was on his own at the time, not having expected to run up against Audie Ringbold, and having gone into a town named Sears Crossing merely to replenish supplies. It had been arranged that he rendezvous with his possemen some ten miles south of that place, from where they were to make for a mine camp known as Corrigan's, where Ringbold had last been heard of, fresh from cleaning out the Sutton Bank and Loan. Conrad, having sent off a telegram to Emmie to apprise her of his present whereabouts, had gone to Lechner's Hotel on Front Street, for a meal.

Conrad sat down at a table and looked up to see Audie Ringbold lounging back in a chair, at another; brand new hat on a peg nearby, snakeskin band, a pair of worsted pants, a flawless white shirt and a blue string tie, a gold watch-chain looped across his close-fitting vest, and a knee-length brown coat. The moment their eyes met, Ringbold grinned, showing his two gold teeth to advantage. An almost handsome man, Ringbold.

'Well now, if it ain't Bob Conrad. Where's the rest o' your blowflies, Bob?'

Conrad had taken up his napkin and had been about to unfold it. Now he placed it, undisturbed, back on the table. There was no evidence of a weapon on Ringbold, but there would be one, under the coat, probably on the left side, handle foremost.

By this time the dining-room staff had sensed that something was wrong, as had some of the other diners, but there must have been uncertainty, at first, as to who these two men were; but by some means it then became frighteningly clear and there followed a careful but singleminded exodus.

'I hope you see sense, Audie, and come in with me.'

Almost idly, Ringbold glanced around. 'Well, Bob, looks like it's just you an' me.'

'This is no good, Audie. It doesn't have to happen. It's best we get up and walk out and go join up with my men. It's over, Audie.'

Ringbold tipped his head back and laughed. 'Bob Conrad. By Christ, this is rich! I hear they roll over an' play dead when they see yuh comin'. Not me though, Bob. It ain't gonna be that easy.'

Conrad sat staring at him. 'I don't want this.'

Ringbold said softly, 'This how it is, Bob, when yuh don't have your boys along?'

'You know better than that, Audie. Well, you ought to know better than that.'

Ringbold was tapping fingers on

the tablecloth. 'Yuh know what your problem is, Bob? Yuh never do smile. Yuh take life too serious. Tell me, how much did they give yuh fer Nate Tanner? I did hear it was ten thousand. Split four ways, two an' one half apiece. An' that was fer the poor bastard dead. They git them other two fer free?' When Conrad said nothing, Ringbold stood up slowly. With his left hand he unbuttoned his coat, let it fall away, exposing the stag handle of a Walker Colt .44. 'So, here we are, Bob. I'll be in the street. When you're ready, c'mon out. Or go out the back way. Your choice.'

★ ★ ★

Dave Dryden appeared through the crowd, though Conrad had seen him coming because of his height, nodding here and there, excusing himself.

'What were they after, Dave? The fillies?'

Dryden, holding a barely-sipped whiskey, glancing around at the gathering, ignored the provocation. 'This ain't my idea of a quiet drink.' Deliberately, he was wearing no sling for his left arm, in which he had taken a ball during the Jago shoot. Conrad believed that Dryden must still be in some discomfort, but that the man would have gone to a rope himself rather than present himself at this gathering as a man wounded in the taking of outlaws. God alone knew what the swarming women would have made of that. As it was, there was bound to be some awkward ceremony. Speeches would be made. The presence of the mayor and other local luminaries guaranteed it. Dryden put a question of his own, perhaps carrying its own pinch of provocation.

'Where's Emmie got to?'

Conrad's gaze had been traversing the big room for the past two or three minutes without locating her. He shrugged. 'Around, somewhere.

Mixing. Doing my share as well, so she thinks.'

Dryden slid him a sidelong look. 'Sam, he ain't popular, neither. Ruth's got some sort of bee in her bonnet.'

From an inner pocket Conrad took a long cigar, and from another, his cutter. Presently, pleasant blue smoke wafted around them.

'I'm goin' on out an' take a walk,' Dryden said, baggy-eyed and defensive. Another man out of his natural element.

'Don't abandon us,' said Conrad. 'We should all be on hand to withstand the full onslaught of Mayor Lithgow.'

Dryden gave a short, choppy kind of laugh and moved away, stiff with social awkwardness. Dryden, in his time, had killed seven men. Conrad thought that the man would do his best in what were, to him, trying circumstances, but if some unsteady celebrant were inadvertently to bump Dryden's hurt arm, the reaction could well be immediate and less than edifying. When that particular and tantalizing thought faded, Audie Ringbold came easing back. That was the trouble, once a man got to thinking, stepping into the trap of reviewing events. The past was populated by ghosts, most of them hostile.

★ ★ ★

When Conrad, in Sears Crossing, came out on Front Street, most of those who might normally have been there, reading the dangerous signs, had taken themselves off. For that matter, there was no immediate sighting of Audie Ringbold either. This was unlikely to mean, however, that he had lit out. Now that he knew that Conrad's men were not in town, he would be feeling confident. Cocky. Thankful that he had not divested himself of the Smith and Wesson Army before going to the hotel for his meal, Conrad opened his coat and swept it back on the right-hand side, to expose the reddish wood handle. Brass shells in his gunbelt shone dully. Conrad went down off the boardwalk onto the dusty street. Ringbold still did not show. Games. Dictating terms. In Conrad's book, all that could ever count was the shoot itself.

Then Audie Ringbold stepped out from behind an unattended wagon outside a mercantile and some eighty feet along Front Street, to Conrad's left.

'Took your time about it, Bob,' called Ringbold. Conrad could have sworn that he could actually see the gold teeth shining.

Without raising his voice over-much, Conrad said, 'Been ordering my meal.'

Ringbold laughed but there was not the same easiness any more. He walked to the middle of Front Street, not hurrying and not taking his eyes off Conrad, who went pacing towards him to close the distance.

'Still not too late, Audie.'

'It is when the choice is 'twixt this

an' a rope.' Before he had quite finished saying it, his right hand was moving with speed for the draw from the left hip. Ringbold got done as cleanly and as quick as anybody, cross-drawing, that Conrad had ever encountered, but even so, it was not quick enough. When Ringbold's Walker was still swinging across to bear, Conrad's lead was hammering him around, sending him stagger-stepping, blood being punched from him under the rolling concussion of Conrad's smoke-wreathed shooting.

★ ★ ★

Laura Maidment said, 'You look done in, Bob. You ought to be somewhere else, taking a rest.' Her very brown, quite large eyes were serious. Concerned.

'This'll be done with soon, Laura. When it is, I'm going away to sleep for three days. Where's Ed?'

'Talking with Mayor Lithgow. Right across the territory, you're the men of the hour, that's quite apparent.'

Again there was nothing insincere about it, nothing remotely sardonic in her tone. But that was Laura. She was a slim, very attractive woman who seemed always to be in calm control of herself.

'This is a real fancy affair,' said Conrad. After a brief pause he said something which, upon reflection, he would never have dreamed of saying to anyone else. Not even Emmie. 'I feel awkward, Laura. I never know what to say to people.'

With feather-lightness she touched his arm. 'Maybe that's no bad thing, looking around here.'

Again Conrad surveyed the scene, the bright colours, the unceasing movement, and listened to the laughter and the tinkling of the music. It sure was a far cry from the scene out on Front Street in Sears Crossing, Audie Ringbold, his pistol fallen away, executing a stiff-legged circle, his eyes wide and protruding, all his light jesting stopped, finally shitting himself when he knew that Conrad was still walking in, holding the long pistol with arm extended, coming to kill him, an ancient stench mixing with the acrid tang of spent powder.

Laura Maidment turned her head. 'Sam Corde is finally about to get his horse ranch, so he tells us.'

'It's been his goal for long enough.'

Laura was studying Conrad. 'And you? And Emmie?'

'We'll see, we'll take a little time, think about it.'

For the space of a moment or two it seemed that Laura would say something more on the subject but apparently changed her mind and said, 'Whatever happens, whatever each of you decides to do, at least the violence is finished with. And you've come through.'

Poindexter of the South Western Railroad, stone-eyed, came forward with a lean hand extended. 'Mr Conrad.'

'Mr Poindexter. You've met Mrs

Maidment, of course.'

'Indeed,' said Poindexter, inclining his head slightly. There was something, though, that seemed to have drawn the railroad man to Conrad, observing him closely and with interest since coming into the room. Only now did Conrad realize what it was that this apparently humourless man saw in Conrad that interested him. It was ruthlessness, recognized in another, no doubt what Poindexter saw as a personal attribute. This sudden recognition gave Conrad a most uneasy feeling.

When Poindexter, his attention engaged by someone else, excused himself, Laura said, 'A very cold man, Bob, Mr Poindexter.'

Conrad did not know how to respond or indeed if he ought to. But briefly, his thoughts slid back to Audie Ringbold, and he found that he had to thrust away the notion that it had not been necessary to keep coming in on Ringbold in the way that he had. For clearly the man had already been disabled and disarmed.

Another silk-soft touch brought Conrad back to the deeply-humming room.

'It's over, Bob, and not before time. You can put it behind you . . . all of you.' The slight pause, the last three words almost tacked on as an afterthought, would also come back to him at a future time. Right now he was astonished at the effortless way in which she had read him. And not for the first time. Ed Maidment was looking in their direction. Laura said, 'I'd best go rescue him.' She moved smoothly away.

Others came and went, most no doubt wanting to be able to say in the future, *I had a private word or two with Bob Conrad.* There was friendliness, yet at the same time a certain reserve, and maybe this was what would endure; for without doubt there would be those who would hold — albeit privately — that Conrad had attracted to himself a disproportionate share of the credit accruing to the group that had acquired his name. As this thought came to Conrad, Sam Corde, at a distance, caught his eye and gave him a distorted grin. It was a glance of instant understanding, and the grin that was only a part of a grin was the same as the one that Corde had given Conrad when the smoke had begun dissipating at Loach's Ferry, the half-breed, Sinde, dead in the river, his blood pinking the moving water, Aaron Bricknell trying to crawl away, the sacks from the South Western express car abandoned, Conrad and Dave Dryden, long pistols wisping smoke, calling upon grievously wounded Billy Niebauer to give up. Billy, though, had managed to get one bloodied arm hooked over the top pole of a corral, horses spooked and circling behind him, hopeless but enraged, prepared to shoot it out, his gnome-face contorted by the intense pain he was in. Niebauer, long pistol still gripped in his right hand, suddenly shot not at Dryden or Conrad (and from where he was, he could not see Maidment) but at Sam Corde, over to his right, the .44 lead actually whipping Corde's hat off his head. Corde, however, stood his ground, levelling his pistol, then shot once, and then again with much deliberation, Billy Niebauer's head whacked savagely, seeming to explode with red spray as he was flung down among the dust and the whirling horses. That had been when Corde had turned his face to Conrad and had given him that ghost of a grin.

In the Shafto House Hotel the food and the drink were still going down in fine style. Vaguely Conrad wondered who was paying for it. This was a matter that had not previously come to his mind. The banks, maybe, though that surely would go against the grain. The railroad? Maybe. He had to concede that banks and railroad together had provided him and his chosen men with the proper incentive to do what they had done; even though they had not quite done all they hoped to have done.

3

Pistols banged and flared again, men called, some running, not easily distinguishable now in the poor light. Some wagons were standing on a loop of bright rails right across from the depot at Renfrew, and against the darkening sky, like a cut-out black card, stood the water tower. In this place there was not a hell of a lot else, very few buildings, a flour mill, a mercantile, as though once, long ago, there had been an impulse to make a town here, followed by a change of mind.

All four of the Conrad Posse were here, and the quick, vicious fight had been going on for the best part of half an hour. Spread out now, they were sometimes cautioning each other about not getting too far out in front. In this quality of light and with this degree of tension there existed a strong possibility of blasting .44 lead into one of your own.

Maybe it was that degree of caution that cost them, in the finish, for when one man managed to get in, quietly, to one of the standing wagons, it was to see that only one of the four men they had believed to be still around here, remained. A cocked pistol at the head of the lone, gaunt, kneeling shooter, brought with it an instant, almost eerie silence; but Conrad, holding the pistol, was in two minds. To call out to his men might be to draw them into crossfire from others still concealed. Shadows were deepening. With the pistol he prodded the kneeling man.

'Stand up. Leave it on the ground.'

This very thin man put his own long-barrelled weapon on the gravelly ground and, joints cracking, got to his feet. 'Yuh'll never git me out, mister. Come sunup, it's you the Goddamn' buzzards'll light on.'

'Walk. Any of the bastards open up now, you'll be the first to Jehovah.'

Conrad could smell the man's rankness and smell his raw fear as well in spite of the boasting. Now Conrad had to risk a call. He licked dry lips. 'Got one here . . . Hold fire . . . ' And again he said, 'Walk.' Thirty yards on, another posseman, Dryden, came out of the gloom near the water tower, the glint of a long barrel evident. 'Which one's this?'

'Ord. Where's Sam?'

'Over yonder.' Softly Dryden called, 'Sam?' There was no answer, but not long after, Corde appeared at the water tower and almost immediately after that, Maidment. Of the man who had been taken and who had now begun coughing deeply, his whole frame seeming to shake uncontrollably, Conrad asked, 'Where are they?'

It was near to half a minute before the coughing ceased and the wheezy breathing of the gaunt man was quite audible. 'Gone. Long gone. Too fly for yuh.' Maybe he could not move as fast as the others.

'Too fly for you, an' all,' said Dryden, behind him, 'by the looks.' But blood was running down Dryden's sleeve.

'Hold him here,' Conrad said, 'while we go take a good look around. If there's any still here, we'll find 'em.'

'Too fly . . . ' said the thin man again, but soon began coughing and was racked by its intensity.

'Only thing that's gonna choke that off,' Sam Corde remarked, 'is the rope they got waiting for you, Ord.'

It was some little while before the captured man could get his coarse breathing enough under control to speak. 'From the time . . . yuh take me in . . . yuh'll never take . . . another step without lookin' to see who's . . . behind yuh . . . '

★ ★ ★

Mayor Lithgow was tapping something on a glass but he had to go on doing it for a while before the humming

38

conversations died enough to leave only the ringing sound he was making. In a raised voice, he said, 'Ladies and gentlemen . . . '

Emmie materialized by Conrad's side, her face flushed and looking a trifle unsettled; but she took his arm. As at a signal, Dryden arrived, too, and Sam Corde and Ruth (she not engaging Conrad's eye) and Ed Maidment and Laura (who did look at Conrad, and smile).

'Ladies and gentlemen . . . I believe it has now come time for me to say a word or two on this occasion — no, this *celebration* — here tonight . . . We welcome Mr Conrad and his, ah, colleagues, Mr Corde, Mr Dryden and Mr Maidment . . . It would not be too much to say that we all have a sense at being present at an important moment in the history of this territory, having moved from a state of near anarchy to what we must all anticipate will be a long period of peace and wellbeing for all who live here and

in the country surrounding Daverne
. . . One by one, the predators who
had for too long preyed upon us, upon
our banks and the railroads, have been
taken, or are dead.' Lithgow cleared his
throat, clearly relishing, as might any
town mayor anywhere, the undivided
attention of a captive audience. Sourly,
Conrad thought that the auguries were
not good. For another thing, every eye
was now turned towards the four tall,
darkly-clad, fiercely-moustached men
and the three undeniably attractive
women standing with them.

'It was widely held,' Lithgow intoned
solemnly, 'that certain of the miscreants
would never be taken, or for that
matter, ever tracked down. I recall
such names as Nate Tanner, Audie
Ringbold, Billy Niebauer and the Jago
brothers . . . '

Ed Maidment glanced at Conrad's
hard-set face. Sooner or later the
Jagos would have been bound to
get a mention. That matter was still
a burr under Conrad's saddle even

though they had taken Ord Jago in Arrowhead.

* * *

When lamps began to be lit some of the crowd that had gathered in the late afternoon was still there, moving around aimlessly, idly scuffing boots, dogs trotting up and down, sniffing, all voices falling flatly on the faint airs of evening. The slack, head-cocked, wrist-bound body of Ord Jago was still turning slowly on the creaking rope below the floor of the raised platform. When the twisting of the rope reached its limit of tightness in one direction, it began revolving its inert burden in the other.

One of the two Jago brothers come to his just reward. So why, somebody at last ventured to ask, was there no dancing in the streets? For stilled, long since, was the deep almost primeval sound that had emerged from the very belly of the crowd that had stretched

41

halfway along the principal street of Arrowhead, occupying, too, every vantage point, every window, every rooftop. The crowd had got what it wanted, what it had ceaselessly changed for. It had seen Ord Jago, who, in the final moments of his life, had managed to spit dangerously at those crowding nearest the raw wood gallows, sent plunging through the trap to eternity. So why *was* there no dancing in the streets? It was almost as though, in the uneasy aftermath, and if such a thing had been possible, they might have called him back. No fewer than four county deputies, one regular and three special, had been on hand up to and during the hanging, spaced at points of vantage, all armed with Winchesters, this against the possibility of Frank Jago, with others, arriving to intervene. That this had not occurred seemed not to have delivered feelings of relief. The probability that by now Frank Jago was more than two hundred miles away seemed not to have penetrated current thinking. James Culpepper who had been with Jago, and Ed Harries who had been with the Jagos had also slipped away, Harries even though it seemed certain that he had been wounded. Conrad had been desperate to come up with all of them but in the end, and blaming no one but himself, had failed to do so.

The possemen who had fetched Ord Jago in were still in Arrowhead. Corde, Maidment, Dryden and Conrad, and a hard-looking lot they were, with their black moustaches, long buff dusters over dark clothing, sour, unsmiling men. Well, hard or not, the now silent men in Arrowhead seemed to be saying that from this day on they had best watch each others' backs, wherever they went, for the more dangerous of the Jagos, Frank, was still alive.

Ord Jago was still turning gently, a new, small breeze sometimes lifting his thinning, coppery hair, his sunken cheeks still flushed with a mockery of health, the overt evidence of consumption. They would burn his clothing, burn the blankets and the mattress from his cot in the jailhouse, then as soon as possible, get him in the ground. But right now, no one seemed prepared to venture near him.

As night drew down, the possemen, now wearing no dusters, darkly dressed, watch-chains looped across buttoned vests, dark blue shirts, black string ties, wide-brimmed, black hats of shallow crown, came walking along the main street of Arrowhead. One of them had his left arm in a black sling.

At the corner of the main street and Aspen, the tall men stood together, light from a pole lamp washing over them, Maidment, Corde, Dryden, Conrad, perhaps now reflecting on success and failure. Just over there hung the mortal remains of Ord Jago.

Fairchild, the Arrowhead County Sheriff, came, stogie glowing cherry red in the gloom, eyes no more than shiny pin-points in the shadow cast by the wide brim of his hat. Mildly, he enquired when they might be moving on. Maidment, his long fingers tucked in his waistband, going up and down on his toes, turned his head slowly.

'Tomorrow, Mr Fairchild, on the noon train. Horses in a boxcar.' He nodded towards Jago. 'My advice is get that blood-spittin' bastard up there off the rope, have *him* put in a box an' nailed down. Don't put off'til tomorrow what you can get cut down today.'

'That's real sound advice, Mr Fairchild,' Dryden said.

'Indeed it is,' said Corde, nodding.

Conrad, a man who made Fairchild's blood run cold, contributed no opinion. All manner of rumours had accrued to Conrad's name, partly because of his reputation as a pistolman, which some said was without peer, and partly because of his unapproachable manner. Rumours about women, too. Some of the rumours would be true, others not. Now, predictably, he was the first of them to turn and go walking away in

45

the general direction of the Frontier Hotel. The other three followed him. Fairchild, baggy-eyed, stood chewing on his stogie. *Noon train, tomorrow.* By God, the sooner the better. Fairchild's thoughts slipped back to the skeletal, wheezing Ord Jago, defiant, sounding threatening even when under restraint and when not racked by his liquid coughing, gasping out his curses, his promises of retribution, spitting at all within range, doing it even as Deputy Teschler pulled the lever. Sentence, long overdue, carried out.

Tomorrow, word having spread around, townsfolk, numerous ladies among them, would find a reason to go by the steamy, oil-smelling depot, observing the hubbub, the straining and slapping and thumping of hooves as the four lean horses were taken up and inside a couple of strawlittered boxcars, the task being carried out by sweating railroad employees, the four big possemen entering a car in the middle of the train. Last sight of them. *'Did yuh see that Bob Conrad? Somethin' to tell your gran'children. But by God, they didn't get Frank Jago.'*

★ ★ ★

Mayor Lithgow cleared his throat. 'One of the Jagos brought back to justice in Arrowhead County, sentenced long ago, but got away that time, the other one, cowed, and abandoned by his cohorts (unlikely, thought Conrad), driven below the border (further guesswork) by the men we have gathered here to honour tonight . . . '

All four possemen were becoming more uncomfortable as Lithgow went on. Enigmatic glances were being exchanged. All this was swamped by applause doubtless fuelled by alcohol. Emmie was leaning somewhat heavily on Conrad's arm.

'Whatever pursuits these brave men now choose to follow, and whatever achievements come their way,' boomed

Lithgow, 'none can surpass the work that they have done in the cause of right thinking over these past months, and at grave personal hazard.' Further applause. 'May I therefore ask you,' said Lithgow, 'to join with me in a toast . . . (a flurry of replenishments) to the Conrad Posse . . . '

The crowd roared, 'The Conrad Posse . . . '

4

Near Sestina, 1882

The bride-to-be was Eloise Croft and she had awakened early. The hour was the one before the first fingers of sun would come probing near her window. The day was still awash with a pale greyness that seemed to have risen out of the earth, leaving objects inside the room and, as she would soon see, the contours of the land outside, still undefined.

As yet no one else was stirring. Even her pa, Daniel Croft, customarily up and about the small farm by this time of day, must still be in his bed. A different day, this. The only daughter of the house was to be wed, and not before time, they were probably thinking. At twenty-five she might easily have been looking at a lifetime of spinsterhood. Now that was all about to change, that particular spectre put to flight. Even though the groom-to-be was more than twenty years older than Eloise.

Slowly, Eloise stirred some more, looking lazily at the faint oblong of the window, the shade only partly drawn. The distance from her home on Pinder Creek to the town of Sestina was no more than six miles, and today the Croft family, Daniel, Hester, Eloise and her younger brother, Thomas, would travel there in the farm wagon, going first to the only hotel in Sestina, the Davis House, where some would change into their Sunday best, Eloise into her wedding dress.

Now there were a few sounds within the homestead, certain rattlings, a door closing. This would mean that the elder Crofts were now up and about. Soon she would hear the clattering of dishes and the sounds of water being pumped up in the little pumphouse in the annexe. Eloise slipped from her bed and crossed to her window and fully raised the old, cracked shade. A morning mistiness and the early hour ensured that all things had a certain formlessness; fences, outbuildings, trees and fields; yet there was about the morning the promise that when the sun rose, this soft distortion of familiar things would be put to flight, and clarity and an enclosing warmth would come flooding in.

Eloise lifted her head. From out of trees near the Sestina trail, dark birds took wing, crows — the countryside seemed alive with them — but almost as soon as the flickering wings were seen they vanished in the greyness. Down there riders were going by, barely heard at this distance and visible only fitfully, grey, bobbing ghosts, three of them, there and then gone. Eloise turned away from the window. It was time to begin her long preparations.

* * *

Elmer Dawson, a Sestina County deputy, stood leaning against an awning post outside the mercantile, building himself a skinny smoke from fresh tobacco, just purchased. The late morning was bright and warm and still, much of the life of the town having been sucked from the streets by the wedding of the Croft girl. Well, girl no more. Woman. Most everybody in this town knew the sodbuster family, a whole lot of people were down at the church, from which dry-boarded place it was possible to hear voices raised in sacred song.

Dawson licked the paper, twisted the end of the quirly and stuck it in his rather small-lipped mouth, then began searching his pockets for a vesta. A brown and white mongrel came sniffing along the edge of the boardwalk, from time to time cocking its leg, but when it saw Elmer standing there it gave him a wide berth before padding in close to the boardwalk again. Street-wise old bastard. Blue, sweet-smelling smoke went wafting away around Dawson's head as he lit the cigarette and flicked the smoke-trailing match into the street. He sniffed, glancing left and then right. Apart from the cautious dog, nothing and nobody was in sight. Dawson yawned. Sestina. Dulltown. Anglewise, to his right, on the opposite side of the street, a bar-dog poked his head out over the top of a pair of batwing doors, saw Dawson and nodded, and the deputy nodded in return.

Inside the crowded church the young woman who had begun the day as Eloise Mary Croft had just left that surname behind, and on the arm of her new husband, had moved into the vestry to sign the register. Not long after that, groom and unveiled bride, linked together, passed slowly along the aisle towards the porch, to where a covered buggy stood waiting, and where there had materialized other townsfolk.

Deputy Elmer Dawson, however, was not among them, still leaning against the awning post, smoking. He was enjoying peace while he could, for there was bound to be a lot of liquor drunk today, and no doubt, numerous scuffles to sort out.

Smiling, to called-out greetings, the bride and groom emerged followed by those who had attended the ceremony, and in pride of place, of course, Eloise's beaming family. So all eyes were on the just-married couple.

When the lashing shot went off, Dawson straightened as though he had been scalded, spun his partly-smoked quirly to the rutted street and, unthonging the hammer of his pistol as he went, began jogging in the direction of the church, where there appeared to be outright chaos. Yet he was hesitant, too, jogging, slowing, jogging on again, for the shot — which had been from a rifle — seemed to have come from another direction, at a distance. But the excitement, the swift scattering of people, was up at the church, women and children screaming as they ran.

The bride, her once pristine white gown spattered with blood, stood screaming too, her hands in long satin gloves pressed to her cheeks. At one instant, standing on the top step alongside her new husband, she had been smiling and speaking to well-wishers, and the groom, Dave Dryden, his face ruddy with pleasure and embarrassment, had been reaching to grasp one of the several outstretched hands. At the next, Dryden's head had exploded with the impact of a .44 rifle bullet, skull punched open like a clubbed melon, blood and brain-matter spraying widely. Down went Dryden as though pole-axed, Eloise flinging herself upon him in her shock and grief, as though performing some absurd act of protection from further hurt. It had taken eight minutes for her to pass from the state of new bride to distraught widow.

Dawson, the deputy, was still coming in a heavy-booted run, pistol drawn, and even as he arrived men were pointing in the direction of a rooftop several streets away. Dawson came to a stop and turned to look. A man was in the act of disappearing downwards, leaving another, a rifleman, still up there, the blur of his face turned towards the church. Though the range was long, the deputy raised his pistol. Calmly the rooftop rifleman sighted and fired, and Dawson, a hole punched in his shirt, in the chest, just left of centre, was knocked backwards and sat down heavily, dying before the dashing echo of the shot had quite gone away.

People were lying everywhere, many with their arms covering their heads as though trying desperately to guard against further danger from above. Some of them had no idea where the shot had come from. The bloodied bride had ceased screaming and, still prostrate over the body of the groom, had fallen to sobbing uncontrollably. The rifleman had gone from the distant rooftop.

Stories later varied as to how many armed men had been seen near an abandoned feed store on Tileman, when two had climbed onto the roof, one of whom had fired a shot and followed that with a second. Three men seemed to be the consensus, and that one man had been holding horses in back of the feed store. This rider had had a gingery beard and much later would be identified as a man named Harries. One of the climbers had been big, thickset, muscular-looking, and brought to mind a certain Culpepper, while the rifleman had been of middle size and very thin, with a prominently-boned face. Whoever they had been they had ridden out fast. By the time the Sestina County Sheriff arrived at the scene of the shooting there was a situation close to panic; and by the time any useful pursuit might have been got under way it was considered to be too late. No one knew in which direction the killers had gone. Anyway, there were few volunteers. And nobody in Sestina had so much as discharged a pistol at murderers who had left behind them two dead men, and one woman whose life had been blighted forever, and all in the passage of a few minutes.

After a little time, however, with both Dave Dryden and Dawson, the Sestina deputy, inside their pine boxes, lowered into the flinty earth, there arose the inevitable speculation about who the raiders had been and why they had singled out — for there could scarcely be any doubt that such had been the case — one man on his wedding day. Gradually, however, remembering who Dave Dryden was — or had been — a member of the famed Conrad Posse, link was added to link until that chain of thought arrived, inevitably, at Frank Jago.

'But that was what, three years back?'

'Dryden was among them that took Ord Jago into Sears Crossin'. Ord was hanged right there.'

'Frank, he got away to Mexico.'

'Yuh know fer sure that's where he went?'

'That was the word.'

'We don't know fer sure it was him that shot Dave.'

'Shot one o' Conrad's men.'

The more it was talked about and thought about the more credible did it become. A teamster passing through the town put his dime's worth in.

'Skinny, bony feller, the rifleman? Jes' like Ord Jago? I seen 'em both, one time, at Lurie's Claim, aw, musta been back in seventy-eight. Skin an' bone, both, an' mean as hoss shit. Sick. Spittin' red, the pair on 'em. Wonder is either of 'em's still ridin'.'

There seemed to be no avoiding the conclusion that Frank Jago, wherever he had been these past three years, had come back. It was as though the hanged man had reached from the grave to seize hold of Dave Dryden and take him there as well.

5

Conrad had a pistol in his hand but did not want to use it, but when two more brawlers began closing in on him, right after he had felled another with a punch, he had started to lay about him with the barrel of the Smith and Wesson.

The saloon was heavy with tobacco smoke that was wreathing blue around the lamps, and boots were sliding on the sawdust-covered floor. The place stank of spilled beer and unwashed humanity. Men were yelling, and probably loudest among them, Ollie Westrupp, who owned this particular saloon. His cries for them to cease, however, were an exercise in futility.

Another backhanded sweep with the pistol caught a near demented, bearded, bull of a man across the bridge of the nose and caused him to go staggering to one side, hands reaching to his bloodied face, roaring in pain. Conrad, with a straight-armed jab, found the throat of the next nearest man with the muzzle of the Smith and Wesson.

There had been a time when merely the sight of Bob Conrad with a drawn pistol would have brought almost instant quiet; and though the mass of half-drunken men in this saloon did now revert to some semblance of order, it was not until Conrad, standing on the bar-top and cocking the pistol, brought a return to reason, and a comparative quiet descended. The three men Conrad had felled were still down in the sawdust in some distress. Conrad stayed up on the bar a little while longer, hatless, in white shirtsleeves with black armbands, still holding the pistol. He waggled the barrel to indicate the three injured men.

'Haul 'em outside. When they can stand, get 'em aboard their horses and see to it they head on out.'

The rotund, bald and sweating

Westrupp was surveying damage to some of his chairs and tables. 'I'll want compensation.'

Grunting, Conrad came down off the bar. 'Not part of my job. You work it out. You know the men that caused this.'

Westrupp gave him a sidelong glance, decided he did not fancy the looks of Conrad's mood and therefore did not press the matter. There had been times when the saloon-keeper and one or two others among the traders in Warbonnet had not been overly subtle in reminding the town marshal exactly who it was who paid his wages at month's end. Maybe the frightening suddenness of the violence and the sight of Conrad's uncompromising way of dealing with it had had a sobering effect on Westrupp, too. For the present.

Conrad stood watching, pistol hanging by his side, as the three hurt men were helped out through the batwing doors, and only then did he put the pistol away and stand for a few seconds, big hands braced against the bar, his black-moustached head hanging, recovering his breath. When he straightened, he picked up his hat which earlier had fallen off, brushed sawdust from it and put it on and left the saloon. His head was aching slightly and he felt older than he had ever felt before.

★ ★ ★

To the small horse ranch under the purple-misted Secordo Hills, while on his way to Tressida County, a man named Vern Coulter brought the news of the death of Dave Dryden.

Sluicing over head and neck water drawn from a stone-rimmed well, then leaning on the heels of his hands shaking his head, spraying droplets like some old hunting dog, he repeated it.

'No saloon rumour, Sam. Been wed no more'n five minutes. County deputy killed an' all. Head-shot, Dave. All hell to pay, there was. Me, I come through there a coupla weeks after. By God, they was still real spooked. Shot down, no chance. Place called Sestina.'

'But who says it was Frank Jago?'

Coulter was wiping one shirt-sleeved arm across his dripping face, blinking from beneath his jutting eyebrows. 'Listen to this. A man about middle height, mebbe fifty year old, thin face, sharp cheekbones, one ear half sliced off. Long jaw. Frank Jago. Gotta be him.'

The man he was telling drew in a long breath and shoved his battered hat back. From the house came sounds of clattering crockery.

'For now, Vern, let it be between you an'me. I'll tell her, but in my own good time.' A pause, then, 'Two men with him. Who? Harries an' Culpepper?'

'Fer sure. Ginger headed, one of 'em.' Coulter was squinting, knowing what must be racing through the other man's mind. 'Cain't know where you're at, Sam. If they did, theyda been here long afore this.'

The response to that came in a much

reduced voice. 'I've had her convinced he'd never come, not now. Not after all this time.' But Frank Jago, having reappeared so suddenly, had got to Dave Dryden. Did it not follow that he would get to others? One by one? It was a big country, but a man as cunning as Jago, once he was on the move, could shrink distances, have eyes and ears everywhere. He could spread fear like the contagious disease that he carried. It was just that, years having gone by, there had arisen a belief that the possibility had long passed.

A woman appeared at the yard door. Ruth Corde, her hair black as a crow's wing, had a small, engaging face. She was ten years younger than her husband. She smiled at Vern Coulter whom she had waved to, briefly, from a window as soon as he had arrived; but the smile had not got as far as her eyes.

'Coffee's ready.'

The men walked towards the house. The woman withdrew inside.

Only after Coulter had ridden on did she begin questioning Sam Corde, and this while they were still out in the yard. 'He brought some bad news. I could tell. That's why he didn't want to look at me. What is it?'

Sam Corde went tramping back inside the house, Ruth following, repeating her question. Corde tossed his old hat onto a chair. 'Dave Dryden's been shot. He's dead.' He would not look directly at her either but knew she had stopped and was standing quite still.

Presently she asked, 'Where did it happen?'

'A helluva long way from here. South-east. Place called Sestina.'

She was reading him now. She had become adept at it after all this time. 'It's that man Jago, isn't it?' Then, 'I knew it would happen, one day, in spite of all you've said. Jago. The one that was supposed to have gone across the border. Or died of consumption, somewhere.'

Now Corde did turn to look at her and saw her ravaged face and began to realize fully the impact that this news had had on her. 'Ruthie . . . '

'Don't even *say* it! You're about to tell me we'll be fine! That he can't possibly find *you*. Find *us*. So how did he find Dave Dryden?'

'I don't know!' It was louder than he had intended, and when the spirit seemed suddenly to drain out of her, he had to step quickly and take hold of her, lest she fall. 'I'm sorry Ruthie . . . I'm real sorry.'

When she next spoke her voice was husky and trembling. 'Sam, we have to leave here. We have to get out of here right now!'

'We can't, Ruthie. Yuh know we can't. All we have is tied up in this place.'

She pushed away from him, not yet in anger, but almost blindly. 'Then we need to get help. We *must* get help.'

Hagen's Crossing was the nearest town, but there was no law to be found in that place. Yet Corde knew quite well what she really meant. She was saying that those who had been part of what she regarded as the mishandling of the Jago enterprise, be called in now to help put it to rights. Uncertainly, worried about her, not about himself, he said, 'I'm not real sure where Ed Maidment's got to. Or Bob Conrad.'

'Conrad.' She repeated the name dully, without passion, yet certainly without warmth. It was plain enough that she viewed the man who had been in charge in going after the Jago brothers as the logical man to carry the responsibility now that they were in what she had come to judge as an awful predicament. For Ruth Corde was in no doubt whatsoever that, because it had been Jago who was said to have murdered Dave Dryden, he would seek out, one by one, the other members of what had been the Conrad Posse. She was moving back and forth restlessly. Corde made as though to take her arm.

'Best you sit down, Ruthie.'

She pulled away from him. 'You'll not soft-talk me, Sam, not about this.'

'All I want is for you to calm down an' let's think what we can do. Vern made a good point. If Frank knows where I am, he'd have been here long before this.' He had not believed Coulter when he had said it and did not believe it now. And he saw at once that Ruth did not believe it either, and that he might well have inflamed the situation rather than dampened it down.

'Vern, with his good points, isn't stuck here, so he won't be around when Jago comes. Sam, you have to get us some *help*!' Now when he took her by the shoulders she did not pull away but allowed him to lead her to a chair. Yet he realized that the news of Frank Jago was by no means the entire story. They had toiled here unceasingly, desperately trying to make a success of it, and the woman had taken her full share of the long, draining hours, and so far for small reward, and the strain of all that had been marked in her face. And now this.

Striving to keep his voice natural, he said, 'Last I heard, Bob Conrad was up around Hainsville. I can go into Hagen's Crossing an' send a telegram, have the telegraph company seek him out, or tell me if it's known where he's gone. Ed Maidment? I just don't know.'

'It was Conrad that held all the opinions about Jago.'

'We were with him as possemen.' When, for a few seconds, she stared at him, he thought she might go as far as some who — though not overtly — had felt at that time that the only thing that was driving Conrad was the big reward on offer. All sorts of rumours and half-truths had abounded, and outright lies. For reasons known only to themselves some people had not been averse to putting Bob Conrad in a poor light. Old memories, old scores, were never far below the surface, strange undercurrents, still running. Conrad himself had warned his possemen. '*You buy into this, you buy into all that.*' The soured, trailing ribbons of old fears, old jealousies, old resentments. Bob Conrad, as much as Ord or Frank Jago, was reckoned to be a man best given a wide berth. Though, up to the present holding back, Ruth Corde was exposing her own festering resentments. Personal.

Corde, unknowing, said, 'All of the blame, if that's what you think it is, can't be laid on Bob. We all knew the risks, but we reckoned on taking both the Jagos. We reckoned we had it laid out real good. But for a poor run of luck, we would have done it, too. Got the pair of 'em.'

'Luck, or judgement?'

Corde could see that her mind was set on denigrating Conrad. Again she stood up and began moving around the kitchen, picking things up, putting them down. He said, 'Tomorrow, first thing, I'll go on into Hagen's Crossing.'

71

It was no more than an attempt at appeasement. Did she not see that, even if he did manage to get in touch with Bob Conrad, and even if Conrad agreed to come, weeks would pass before there was any sight of him? Of course, there was the extreme option of persuading Ruth to go with him into Hagen's Crossing, she, from there, to take the stage north while he came back here to wait out, alone, this uncertain, perhaps dangerous time. Corde stopped short of putting that forward, knowing the kind of response it could well provoke. He had misjudged how close to the border of unreason she now was, and in a certain sense, this seemed even more disturbing than the news of Dave Dryden, the appalling details of his sudden death.

So, as good as his word (though the sight of his preparations seemed not to have lightened Ruth's mood) Corde saddled up and, in the quiet morning, headed away towards the faint trail that eventually would lead him to the town of Hagen's Crossing. The big bay horse under him was eager for a run, and for the first half mile, Corde gave it its head, then eased it down.

The distant sound of a rifle shot caused him to draw rein and bring the bay to a side-heaving halt, the horse blowing strongly and wagging its head. Corde sat half turned in the saddle, listening, and looking back the way he had come. The rolling country lay still under the sun, but for one flickering of movement. Far back, some birds had risen, and against the horizon's chalk-mark of cloud, were fast vanishing into the haze of distance. One shot and quick bird-rise. Unseen fingers were clawing at Corde's belly. He made himself wait. There came no further sounds of shooting.

They must have just missed finding him there, but knew that he would come back to that one shot. Corde turned the horse around and headed back to where he had left Ruth, alone.

In the hour before sun-up, in the grey hour, Conrad, dressed so far in only undervest and pants, stood staring out of his open, upper window, across the sorry-looking roofs of the town. His left hand was swollen, the rawbone knuckles skinned, and it was now paining him. It was far from a disabling injury but he knew that the annoyance of it would be a throbbing presence for maybe the next couple of days. And the partly-drunk lump of itinerant shit that he had walloped with it had scarcely been worth the trouble; but in the circumstances there had been no option, a pistol about to be drawn. It had all ended in that welter of broken chairs and tables, and later, somebody vomiting into the sawdust under the smoky lamps. Bob Conrad, come down to this, quelling yet another saloon brawl in a place that looked like the ass-end of nowhere. Town marshal. Christ.

Behind him, the bed that once had been not only his but Emmie's lay rumpled, an indentation on only one of the pillows. Disconsolately, Conrad continued regarding the jumble of dirty rooftops, one of them covering the site of last night's violence. The Red Dog Saloon. Ollie Westrupp's. There had been a time when Conrad would have brushed aside the likes of Westrupp with scarcely a glance, save perhaps one that gave out an unmistakable caution to stay clear. True, even now, he gave Westrupp, and others, reason to believe that if he had Conrad's services at his disposal, there was not a garnering of respect to go with it. The brutal truth, however, was that Conrad, in middle age, was sorely in need of the money. There had been reasons for that, of course, not least among them, Emmie. With her had gone nearly all of the money that he had put by, the fruits of extreme risk-taking, rewards for lawfully having brought in felons, and some compensation for having had lead dug out of his body on three occasions. A whole world away, now, was the gathering two weeks after the hanging of Ord Jago. It had been in that plush hotel in Daverne, one final coming together before they went separate ways, Conrad, Maidment, Corde and Dryden, and the numerous good-looking women in their bright dresses. It had been a world that Conrad would not see again.

He turned from the window and crossed to the wash-stand, and from a bowl there sluiced stone-cold water over his face and neck, then dried himself on a threadbare towel. He lifted a blue shirt from one of the brass bedposts and, some-what stiffly, put it on. He needed more sleep, but knew now that having been on his feet for a time, it would be pointless to go back to bed. A strange mood had come upon him when, for no reason, he had started awake in the early hours, and had been unable to rid himself of a growing apprehension that, equally, he had been unable to explain. But it had persisted and that had been why he had got out of bed and got partly dressed. The chill that he now felt was more than that present in the air of early morning, like a chill of the spirit, another turn of the wheel, perhaps, the product of an ageing mind and body.

* * *

To go rushing in was Corde's first desire, but reason borne of other days gave rise to caution. A hundred yards short of the spread of low-pitched buildings and the numerous corrals where the brood mares were, Corde, screened by a stand of cottonwoods, drew rein, he slid from the saddle, unscabbarding the Winchester as he did so, leading the bay horse forward, hitching it to a low-bending branch. Corde levered a round into the chamber and walked almost to the fringe of the trees, his attention fixed on the ranch-house.

The first significant thing was that, if he was right, if they were here, their horses were nowhere to be seen. But, just as something had startled the birds that he had observed from a distance, perhaps the same thing had led to a fluttering of chickens in the yard, and they were still not settled. Then somewhere, and not very far off, a horse whickered. Corde had just decided to quit the trees, but instead of going directly towards the house he would go around in a wide circle and make his approach through one of the corrals.

He had taken the first step when he heard Ruth scream, the sound cut short as though she might have been struck. Corde's skin crawled as he stood still, gripping the rifle. For a few seconds there was quiet, then Ruth began screaming again, and this time the sounds went on and on, and she was shrieking his name. 'Sa-am . . . ! Sa-am . . . !' But by now she must have known it was useless.

Corde swallowed, sweat-slick and breathing hard, eyes closed, until it became too much and he did what every instinct warned him he should not do, but what those inside the house hoped he would do. Corde broke cover and, rifle held in both hands, went in a swaying run towards the house, wanting only to get there and make those dreadful sounds cease and kill the men who were in there with her.

At the house, glass was punched out of a window-frame, and he had the quick impression of an arm and a long-barrelled pistol. It blasted at him and lead wafted close as he came on. Though he did not realize it, he was shouting obscenities at them, trying to close the distance fast, knowing quite well what was occurring inside the house. A form appeared at the window from which the pistol had now been withdrawn, but now, in the yard doorway, pistol levelled, stood the bony shape of Frank Jago, pale, thin legs spraddled as he took aim, Frank clad in nothing but his dirty blue shirt. The pistol bucked and smoked and Corde was hit and went down, but at the same time triggering a shot at Jago, which missed, flinging slivers of wood from the doorframe. Somehow Corde managed to get to his feet again. Ruth was still screaming. Too late, Corde glimpsed someone over to his right, near the wagon-shed. He could not have known that, as well as Culpepper and Harries, Frank Jago had acquired two other men who had ridden with him in the past, by the names of Walsh and Avery, and it was Walsh who now drew down on him. Corde stood no chance, and though half turning, he fired at Walsh and nicked him, was himself driven down on his knees, lead whacking into him, so that when he tried to raise the rifle again, suddenly it weighed a hundred pounds, and anyway he was blinking his eyes in a wet, red veil; and then in absolute darkness.

When, hours later, hoofbeats fading

in the calm morning, Ruth came crawling, naked, battered and trailing blood across the floor of the kitchen, to the yard door, there was only a shape out in the yard, under whirling and seething flies. Still on her hands and knees, it took her another five minutes to cover the distance, head hanging, her lips swollen and her bruised eyes staring, and when, finally, she reached him, she found that he was beyond her, now, crumpled and bloodied. And sodden, one or more of them having paused to piss on him.

6

It pained her to watch him fighting not to show his pain, but as day followed day it was becoming patently obvious that his strength was leaving him. Because he could no longer stand quite straight, and he had lost weight, his entire frame seemed to have diminished. Once more than six feet in height and looking it, broad shouldered and barrel chested, physically powerful, Ed Maidment nowadays appeared to be a different man entirely. After a horse, spooked by a savage dog, had first thundered its rider against the poles of a corral, then emptied him out of the saddle, to fall awkwardly, those who had come running to Maidment had thought him dead. Indeed, he had not been far from it, and months had gone by before — and then only with the aid of two sticks — he was able to take a few hesitant steps. Over time, though steadier on his feet, he had not progressed much beyond that.

They had been in partnership with a man named Lowndes, in a mercantile venture, in a town called Saffron when the accident happened, and it had seemed to be the very worst luck they could have had. It had not been quite the worst, however, for even while Maidment had still been flat on his back, Lowndes had vanished, along with the bulk of their joint funds. Soon enough, creditors were banging on the door, and ultimately the business had been lost. Laura had done her best. She had put her mind to clearing every debt, but to do it, the mercantile had had to be sold. The Maidments had emerged, the man badly crippled, with a fraction of the money they had started out with.

Through all of this, Laura Maidment had revealed the true strength of her character, managing the awkward business of the debts and the disposal of the mercantile, and then, because they had had to seek a less costly place to live, arranging their move to a smallholding just a few miles from the town of Stoller, on the Torrey River. There, it was their plan to grow most of their own food and to trade their surpluses in Stoller in return for other needs. To a certain degree it had worked out, but in their second season there had been a drought, and this had come about at the same time that Ed Maidment had had to take to his bed again for several weeks, emerging in a weakened state and thus unable to work full days around the property. Laura had thereupon sought employment in Stoller and had waited tables at the Criterion Hotel and worked behind the counter in a dress shop. They were getting by, but only just.

Now, however, there had come to them — chiefly through things overheard by Laura while working at the Criterion — that Dave Dryden, one of the famed Conrad Posse, was dead, and so was another of them, Sam Corde.

Maidment was slumped in a wide, creaking cane chair in the corner of the homestead kitchen. The disjointed stories of the killings and the brutal raping of Ruth Corde had had a visible effect on the ailing man, his face slackening and turning a greyish colour. It was as though he had aged even as his wife had been looking at him. Presently, Maidment asked, 'What's become of Ruth?'

'I don't know.' Laura had never been close to Sam Corde's wife, and indeed had not found a great deal to like in the woman. Now, however, the horror of what had happened to Ruth Corde brought only a feeling of compassion.

Maidment asked, 'The people in town, do they connect us with Conrad?'

She shook her head. 'At this distance, and after all this time, they seem to be only repeating things that have been said. I doubt that many of them had even heard of Dave, or

Sam, before this.' Then she said, 'He found them. Jago. If he found *them* he could find *us*.'

Ailing he might have been but his mind was not afflicted. 'If they questioned Ruth, maybe she'd have known we were in Saffron. Now we're some way from Saffron.'

'We made no secret of where we were heading. We had no reason to.'

'It's long odds, Laura, that he'd track us to Stoller.'

She knew that he was trying to offer her reassurance and suddenly she resented it. 'Don't talk to me as though I'm a child, Ed.' He was somewhat taken aback, not only by the remark but by its tone. It was unlike her, perhaps revealing the true measure of her concern, and before he could respond, Laura went on, 'If he does come we're not in any shape to defend ourselves.'

'I'll not go crawlin' to the law!' She knew perfectly well that he did not hold a high opinion of Keswick, the Torrey County Sheriff.

'I wasn't thinking of Troy Keswick. I meant Bob Conrad.'

'No.' Maidment shook his head. 'Keswick. Conrad. I'll not demean myself. An' I'll not *be* demeaned, Laura.' This was a flash of the Maidment of old, the tall, almost at times menacing figure, the shadow behind the shell now slumped in the cane chair. He was giving her warning that the once-known Maidment still existed, inside the shell. The disability had failed to kill him off. 'Hear me?'

'I do hear you, Ed.' Yet that did not mean that the spectre of Frank Jago had vanished. Tight lipped, Laura went about household tasks. Maidment fell into one of his increasingly frequent, black, clamp-mouthed moods. The nature of the demons ranging the borders of his mind at these times, she would never know. Long before this, she and Maidment had reached a stage of long silences, finding less to talk about. It was as though the intimacy of other days had been something between two entirely different people. Now, he needed help, so she helped him; but only ever to the point at which he could manage for himself. To persist beyond that point, no matter how well intentioned she might be, was to invite a sharp rebuke.

Laura bided her time, but when next she was in Stoller, so arranged matters that she encountered Sheriff Keswick. Courteous enough, his round face with its reddish sideburns, bland, as soon as she mentioned the name Frank Jago, the lawman's eyes shifted uncomfortably. Yes, it did happen that he had heard of the death, somewhere, of Samuel Corde. And of Dave Dryden, on his wedding day. For a peacekeeper, however, Keswick's attitude was an odd one.

'What's done is done, Mrs Maidment. Sometimes it means there's things that are left hangin' (not seeming to use the term in a mischievous sense) so it won't be surprisin' if there's some other bad things come out of it.'

It must have been obvious to him that she was dismayed. 'Mr Keswick, I'm surprised that you find what Jago has done a natural outcome of what were lawful enterprises.'

'Look here, Mrs Maidment, I got a sworn duty to keep the peace in this county, but if Jago is drawn here, there'd be only one reason, an' not one o' my makin'.'

Choking back bitterness, she said, 'Are you telling me that you'd not lift a finger?'

'Didn't say that. If Jago comes, an' if he causes me trouble, then I'll have to take a hand.'

She could perceive, though, that it was a soft statement, one of a kind that Ed Maidment would have claimed you could have driven a wagon through, with a six-horse team. She could also see that to pursue the matter any further with Keswick would be pointless. Whether he was aware of what men would in all likelihood be travelling with Jago, she did not know, but to raise that, now, she felt might look like pleading, but she did say, 'In no way did my husband wish me to come seeking help. I chose to go against his wishes. Now I can understand what it was that he knew, and that I didn't.' She left Keswick with his mouth open and his face flushed and with the realization that she had seen through him.

Laura went to the telegraph office and sent a telegram to the last place she and Ed had thought Bob Conrad to be, a town called Hainsville. Her cryptic message recorded the deaths of Dryden and Corde, thinking that Conrad might be in ignorance of them, and the consequent vulnerability of the injured and ailing Maidment. In some sort of deference to her husband she added that the sending of the message was entirely her own doing, finishing with the one word which she believed would say everything to Conrad. Pride.

★ ★ ★

Ed Maidment came walking awkwardly across the hardpack of the yard, leaving the cavernous barn, making his way through numerous pecking chickens. His progress was slow and awkward, assisted by two stout lengths of hickory, several painful steps followed by a pause, then an effort of will, to manage a few more paces. During each of the pauses Maidment turned his head this way and that, narrowed eyes studying the country all around. He knew that he had allowed the long-vanished Jago to invade his waking hours, and knew, too, that this would be a part of the payment that Jago was now exacting from what was left of the Conrad Posse that had ridden so hard and so far and in its time had been thought to be invincible. Hard, uncompromising men, men of the sort that had been needed to confound and confront others who had been every bit as hard. Brutal. Sourly, Maidment reflected that the once-proud riders, a group that had been gathered together quickly, had flourished spectacularly, but briefly, and in the measure of the three years following that night of celebration in the Shafto House Hotel in Daverne had, in their disbandment, withered away, and quite soon might vanish altogether, and thereafter, scarcely be remembered. Frank Jago might well be the one who would be remembered longest.

Clumsily he negotiated the porch steps and passed inside the homestead to slump into the big cane chair, breathing out noisily with relief. If they could but see him now, he thought, those who had known him in his prime, they might well pass him by, unrecognized. This surely could not be the man who, before the advent of the Posse, as far back as '76, and for bounty, had come for Jack Vargas at the settlement along the foot of the Miranda Hills, the place of the mad-eyed evange-lists and the child-wives, bearded, oaf-Messiahs, shouting their imprecations, promising the darkly-clad rider a fiery retribution if he did not turn away. All to give Jack Vargas time to bolt from one of the sad soddies, running towards the river, clad only in pinkish longjohns and carrying a Peacemaker.

Vargas did not reach the river, for Maidment had not dismounted, and forty yards short of the water, turned to shoot. But the hurried escape from the soddy and the run through the bunch-grass had cost him, and Vargas, whose reputation said that he seldom missed, did so. Not by much, for Maidment had been conscious of the heavy lead whipping by. But Maidment, even from a moving horse, shot Vargas, hitting him twice, each hit slapping dustily at the longjohns, as though the garments had been filled with kapok.

Yet that had been but one incident in years of violent confrontations, not the least of which, those connected with the Conrad Posse. Briefly Maidment thought about Conrad and wondered if indeed he was still up around Hainsville. Then soon — and again — his thoughts slid to Laura. Still with him. Bitterly Maidment wondered how much of an influence in that was the fact of his disability. For there could be no avoiding the cold truth, they had been drifting apart, him and Laura. It was still a matter of some bemusement to him, now that for an unforseen reason he had more hours in the day to brood, that a woman like Laura had ever given him a second glance. When this thought again crossed his mind on this solitary day, he wondered if that was not a contradiction, for he had also had time to brood over the possibility that Laura might have found an attraction elsewhere. If she had — and he had no evidence whatsoever — then in these western lands the object of her interest was unlikely to be a man of culture, a cut above the pistolman that inescapably Maidment was. Had been. A doctor though? An attorney? By Maidment's recollection, Laura had had few opportunities during the years he had known her, to meet such professional men; and the ones that he could recall had surely been of a sort to have had little appeal. Long ago he had confronted himself with the unpalatable notion that he, and he alone, was the reason for her discontent. Searching for the possibility of someone else, some shadowy presence, was no more than an excuse for personal failure. In his dire circumstances, to harbour thoughts such as these served merely to exacerbate his feelings of frustration and the impotent anger that sprang from it.

Painfully, Maidment, gripping his sticks, hauled himself out of the creaking chair and made his way through to the bedroom, a room, even in her absence, filled with her presence; creams in jars, bottles of perfume, a cleanliness and orderliness which seemed strange in such a remote and raw environment. Maidment laid aside his sticks and opened a drawer in his own bureau. He lifted out a long, rakish pistol, a Colt .44, a holster and a thickly-shelled belt, cloths and gun-oil, and these he carried, shuffling, to the kitchen and dumped them on the table. He was capable of moving for short distances without the aid of the sticks, but now struggled, going back to the bedroom to retrieve them.

Compelling himself to concentrate on the job in hand, Maidment stripped and cleaned the pistol, then thoroughly tested the mechanism and finally loaded the weapon, having examined each of the new loads before pressing it home in the cylinder. Hardly had he finished this task when at a sound, his head lifted. The buckboard was being driven into the yard. Laura.

7

The familiar streets, the false fronts and the corrals and storehouses of Hainsville had done nothing to stir feelings of pleasure in the mind of Emmie Naver. There was much less of a sparkle to her eye now, and perhaps a belated and secret regret that she had acted without due thought. It was not that she was contemplating returning to Warbonnet, even on the slimmest of chances that Conrad might welcome her. The man was unforgiving of manifestly smaller transgressions, and what she had now done must have seemed to the dark-moustached, dark-mooded man, a final humiliation.

Attracted by a land deal in country near Warbonnet, they had gone there — she, willingly enough at that time — but it had all turned sour. Even as conservative a man as Bob

Conrad could find himself on the wrong end of a deal where a substantial sum of money was involved, and where an attorney proved to be less than honest. Financially it had been disastrous, and that had been the real reason for the rift between them. She had tended to blame him — unjustly, so he had claimed — and it had been this that had driven the real wedge between them. From that point, too, there had been a revival of her other activities. Other men. Conrad, having had to take whatever work he could find, eventually becoming the town marshal in Warbonnet, placing him at the beck and call of men who, in better times, he would have had no dealings with, had been away from their home a good deal, particularly at night. Which, too, often, had left the vulnerable Emmie to her own devices, lonely, increasingly frustrated and resentful.

There had arrived a whiskey drummer from the mid-west, or so he had said, and, leaving town separately, a promise to meet her in Hainsville, to travel east from that place. (*We'll make a real fine pair, Emmie, you an' me.*) So, by railroad, to Hainsville she had gone, a note left behind for Conrad, but discreet observations and enquiries in the town where she had once lived had failed to turn up hide nor hair of the drummer. And though one or two of the many people in Hainsville who knew her might have wondered what had brought her there without Conrad, her coming seemed to have excited no special interest. The very fact that she was well known to be Bob Conrad's woman had been in all likelihood sufficient to keep at bay any who might have been curious.

Having taken a room in a house on Galliard, there to ponder what her next move should be, Emmie was now passing along the boardwalk on Front Street, colourful parasol up, looking in store windows. Repeatedly, however, Conrad intruded into her thoughts, as she recalled his tense, quick anger when, slightly fuddled with drink, she had accused him of duplicity in his association with Ruth Corde.

'We all knew she wanted you. She couldn't hide it. Only poor old Sam couldn't see it. Sam couldn't see anything, except *her*.'

'That's all a Goddamn lie, Emmie. There was nothing, ever, between me an' Ruth.' To be accused in this way, remembering the blunt rebuff he had handed Ruth, and the clear malevolence of the woman, that followed on the heels of it, was galling and provoking to Conrad. And this atop all that had happened in recent years, culminating in a betrayal of trust, over land, in the grimy place in which, paid by men who were far from his betters, he was reduced to dealing with itinerant, often dangerous drunks. It had seemed to Conrad to be the final humiliation. He had not struck her — he had never struck Emmie — but she knew that he must have come close to it on that night. Emmie herself did not know whether or not there *had* been anything between him and Ruth Corde, with the certainty that only another woman could have known, that at one stage at least, Ruth had been ready and more than willing and had not been reticent in demonstrating it.

Lifting the hem of her pale green skirt, Emmie had just crossed an intersecting street and stepped up on the next boardwalk when, at a call, she stopped and turned. Like others in Hainsville, Gittings, the telegraph operator, had never been sure of how he ought to address her. *Mrs Conrad* was not it, while *Miss Naver* did not seem appropriate either, so the man who was hurrying to catch up with her now, simply said, 'Mrs . . . uh . . . Mrs . . . ' Emmie, waiting, gave him a small, twisted smile. He was waving a yellow flimsy. 'Got a telegram.'

'For me?' God, maybe it was from Conrad. Somehow she did not think it would be from the drummer.

'Uh, no ma-am . . . ' (safe ground here) 'for Mr Conrad. Somebody musta figured he was still around Hainsville.'

'Well, Mr Conrad is not with me on this visit,' Emmie said smoothly, but quickly added, 'But I shall be seeing him soon.' She had extended a green-gloved hand for the message.

Gittings hesitated. 'I could relay it on to Warbonnet, ma-am. Ain't no trouble.'

'Much less trouble for me to hand it to him.' Emmie said. She was curious to learn who might be sending a telegram to Conrad, and why. Maybe it would provide some kind of lever she could use. Maybe, she thought, it was from Ruth Corde.

Very slowly, clearly uncertain, the telegraph man handed her the yellow slip. She grasped it, nodded, smiled brilliantly at him and turned away. Outwardly in no hurry, but intrigued to know what was in the message, Emmie continued her casual progress along Front Street, occasionally nodding a greeting as she saw a familiar face; but she did not pause to talk with anyone for she did not want to have to answer questions about why she might be in Hainsville and where Bob Conrad was.

Soon, however, she made her way back to the rooming-house. Once in the seclusion of her room, her hat and gloves removed, she opened the folded flimsy and read the message. Even after she had finished she stood quite still and read it through again, the words seeming to drum inside her head. Surely it was not possible. Dryden, dead. And at his wedding? Corde, dead. Ruth Corde in a bad way. That could mean just about anything. Shot? Assaulted? Maidment, not found yet, but a cripple. Jago. *Jago*. Again that name came jumping out at her. But it was not Ed Maidment who had sent what was plainly a plea for help, and it was equally clear why. The telegram was explicit enough on that point, to anyone who had met the man. Or any of them. *Pride*. That word also stood out on its own. The message was signed Laura. And it was perfectly clear that Laura believed that Bob Conrad would come running. But come running for the sake of Ed Maidment, or for the sake of Ed Maidment's wife? By the end of the fourth reading Emmie could have recited the entire message. In due time, through word of mouth and through newspapers, these events were sure to become common currency, even as far away as this. But for the present it was information which she alone would possess, here and probably in Warbonnet.

Quietly she made her way downstairs to where the kitchen was. No one was around, but the stove was glowing. Emmie fed the light yellow paper in and watched it curl and brown and vanish in sudden flame.

⋏ ⋏ ⋏

Of course the newly-cleaned pistol had been the first thing that Laura had noticed when she had come in. And at his behest, and in silence, she had brought his Winchester to him, and he had thoroughly cleaned and checked that weapon as well. Later, however, supper over, she had managed to penetrate his dour wall of silence.

'I've talked with Trudy Hayes, because there's nothing for me, right now, at the hotel. I can help out three days in her shop, starting tomorrow.' A milliner's.

Ed Maidment barely looked up, and not without betraying some degree of bitterness, said, 'I know you've got to carry me. Carry us. But I'm damned if I like you havin' to go back an' forth on your own.'

'Ed, there's no way around that.'

He gave a small gasp and shifted in his chair, the cane creaking sharply. 'There's another pistol around somewhere that you could work. I can find it an' clean it an' you can take it along.'

She shook her head. 'And do *what* with it? Ed, can you really see me using it?'

'Then I'd best come along.' As soon as he had said it he realized how absurd it was, imagining hanging around in Stoller, being observed, talked about, in a place which, in any case, he deeply disliked. Since his accident he had learned to his dismay and his anger that now there were people around who seemed almost to relish the fall of one of the great Conrad Posse, an attitude which Maidment had never even begun to understand. Although the work of Conrad and his men had been carried out a long distance from this part of the country, their names and what they had achieved were widely known. Maidment by no means sought privilege on that account, and indeed had felt as ambivalent about the euphoria and adulation in Daverne in '79 as had Conrad himself, but at least he believed that every man who had ridden with Conrad back then was due a certain respect wherever he happened to be. Yet the unaccountable fickleness, even unfairness of public perception was something that Maidment had found as bitter as gall.

As so often happened nowadays, their talk soon fell to silence, yet it was a silence still loaded with old misunderstandings, the worse for their not being brought out into the open again. Laura busied herself with numerous tasks and on the following morning drove the buckboard into town and did her day's work in Trudy Hayes' shop. After she had taken a break for a meal in one of the Front Street cafés she visited the telegraph office. The operator shook his head. No message for Mrs Maidment. Next day the answer was the same; and the day after that.

Slowly Laura walked back to the milliner's shop. Now she had to confront more than one possibility. Conrad was no longer in Hainsville; or he was, but he had chosen to ignore her. The second was hard for her to take, for she had come to believe that Bob Conrad genuinely respected her. More, that he liked her. At the very least she had been sure that the courtesy he had always shown her would not simply have vanished into the air. That was not Conrad's way, of that she felt sure.

That third day at the shop was a busy one, but during the afternoon, Laura, sweeping the floor, then brooming out onto the boardwalk, noticed that, diagonally across Front Street, Sheriff Keswick had emerged from his office at the county jail. He was not looking pleased. A black-whiskered man whom Laura recognized as one of the deputies, had come out also. Both stood looking towards the far end of Front Street. The plump woman, Trudy Hayes, came out to where Laura was.

'Something going on?'

'I'm not sure.' There did not appear to be any kind of disturbance.

Sheriff Keswick, noticing Laura on

the opposite side of the street, apparently not having forgiven her for her comments a few days ago, gave her a brooding look, then went pacing along the boardwalk with his deputy.

Not long after that, a man passing said to the two women outside the shop, 'Ol' Kes on the prowl. Couple o' drifters up at the Yeller Dog, throwin' it back, givin' Olroy a hard time. Look real mean. One of 'em's a feller named Culpepper, an' by his looks, I sure wouldn't want to cross 'im.'

The name drove at Laura like a knife. The man, who had now walked on, might have seen no significance in it, nor might Sheriff Keswick, but Laura had heard about Culpepper often enough, from her husband. Where Culpepper was, Jago would not be far away.

With Trudy Hayes, she walked back in the shop. The late afternoon had not been busy. After a little while, mechanically tidying shelves, she suggested to the milliner that there was really little point in her working the full day. 'Ed's not been too well. Maybe I should go on back and see he's all right.' Trudy Hayes had no objection. The good news, as far as Laura was concerned, was that the men who had been causing concern up at one of the saloons had ridden out, and clearly they had gone in the opposite direction from the one she must take, on her buckboard.

8

Even the act of startling birds from the trees as she drew nearer to the homestead assumed an ominous aspect, the urgent rushing of wings startling her, so tense had she become. For the late afternoon was hushed, offering a sense of timelessness across the vast tracts of this raw country, a country in which individuals were diminished, reduced in importance within the greater scheme of things.

In the nearer distance she could see, now, between the trees, the sharp angles of the farm buildings. Familiar, yet in an odd way, today not a welcome sight, not in the least a sense of *this is home*, or, *here is sanctuary*. Never before had she experienced such an alien sensation about this place, anxious to arrive, yet dreading it, so approaching it for the purpose of release from the dreadful tensions of *not knowing*. Fearing the worst. Trudy Hayes had suspected that something was wrong, and Laura had come close to confiding in the other woman, yet in the end had held back.

She drew the buckboard to a stop. She could see no sign of Maidment in this stillness of the day. The shadows were lengthening. The silence was unnatural. Reluctantly she walked the pair forward, soon coming to the spacious yard. The chickens were pecking around and there was a startled fluttering as she drove the buckboard in.

'Ed . . . ?' Her voice sounded flat, diminished, as again she drew to a stop and this time got down.

Inside the house he was nowhere to be found. Moving hesitantly, calling, Laura passed from room to room, still getting no answer. The unresponsive quiet itself seemed to take on an aspect of a menacing reply. A new apprehension clutched at her. In one of the rooms, propped in a corner, she saw the Winchester. Laura reached and picked it up and sniffed at it. Oil. No sharp tang from its having been fired in recent times. Briefly she considered carrying the weapon with her but in the finish put it back where she had found it. Now, her heart beating strongly, she went back outside. Fixing her eyes on the barn she crossed the yard and entered that straw-smelling cavern, looked around, then went up into the loft. Nothing. Slowly she descended and once more stepped into the yard.

There were numerous smaller out-buildings. One by one she went to them, pushed open old doors, looked inside. Again, nothing. Wherever he was he could not have gone far, even if he had heard them coming at some distance. Yet he had not taken up the rifle. That being so, had he been outside and not able to reach it in time? For with a leaden heart she believed — no, she *knew* — that they had been here. Though she had seen not a shred of evidence, she thought she could almost *smell* their recent presence. What, undeniably she could smell was the sharpness of woodsmoke.

Sixty feet away from where she was, was a clump of trees. To reach them she must cross a patch of thick bunch-grass. Laura lifted the hem of her light-brown skirt and headed across towards the trees. Only a few feet from them she stopped abruptly. In the long grass lay one of Ed Maidment's sticks. Now real fear did grab at her belly. Instantly, hope against hope vanished.

Compelling herself to move on, she went by the fallen stick and in among the trees. As she now knew it would be, there lay the second stick. She stood looking down at it intently as though expecting it to provide her with answers. A further two paces. Then she found him.

Ed Maidment was tied to a tree. Or what was left of him. Laura closed her eyes and turned away, suddenly vomiting, and after the spasms had subsided, remained head down for several minutes, hands propped on her knees. Eventually she made herself straighten and look again.

There was no sign of the Colt pistol. Perhaps they had taken it. In the last minutes, Maidment must have tried to get away, and falling, tried to crawl. Hopelessly. Whatever had gone on, his end had been horrific. Arms pulled back on either side of the tree-trunk and tightly secured with leather thongs that had cut deeply, bloodily into his scrawny wrists, he had been stripped naked, the veins in his limbs like blue rivers, his skin, where it remained untouched, an unhealthy, milky colour. What remained of the fire was some few feet away, still wisping smoke out of white, redcored ash.

There was no bullet hole to be seen. They had burned him badly, systematically, and probably over an extended period. On his crippled legs, on his belly and his genitals, in his groin and his armpits and his ears. And they had burned his eyes out, leaving two seared, black-rimmed, reddened caverns above a face that, in death, still retained its rictus of appalling agony, lips pulled back from the teeth, mouth still open in a silent, eternal scream.

How *shrunken* he looked. Until not so long ago, this had been a man of above six feet in height, muscular, broad of shoulder, a commanding presence, as had been each one of the legendary group, the Conrad Posse. Yet here were his pathetic remains. Here was the silent recounting of his final agonies. In the end, had the strong man pleaded with them? Had they broken him, denied him the last shreds of that quality — or was it fault — that she had named in her telegram to Conrad? *Pride.*

Though in recent years there had been a sensitive gulf between them — perhaps it had nearly always been there — he had been her husband, so it was impossible for her to feel *nothing*. And no creature, whether human or not, deserved what had been done to Ed Maidment. Yet she found that she could not bring herself to touch him.

Laura turned away. Tomorrow, for at this moment she could not face the journey, she would make the trip back into Stoller and arrange for an undertaker to come out here; and Sheriff Keswick or one of his deputies, just so they could see for themselves just what Frank Jago was capable of. She hoped that Keswick himself would come. Jago. Laura wondered where that man had been when Culpepper had been in Stoller; for she believed that he had not been the other man, with Culpepper. With a dreadful feeling of vulnerability, she wondered then if he might have remained near here, wanting to see her reaction. Fearfully she looked all around her, but nothing stirred and the silence of the remote place ran on.

Conrad's name came flying back to her. The last of the posse that had borne his name. Surely Jago's last, and most highly prized target. Her mind was racing. *Oh, God, Bob, where are you?* Fingertips pressed to her temples, she found that she was walking across the hardpack of the yard, and now, out of horror and confusion, one or two sane notions were beginning to come to her. Possibilities.

★ ★ ★

Sometimes riding with Frank Jago, sometimes not, Walsh and Avery were back with him, along with Ed Harries (who had been slightly wounded during the fight, years back, when Ord Jago had been taken) and James Culpepper. They had fetched up in a dump called Sturrock, full of nondescript structures left over from more prosperous times, dead-eyed, workless men and their scrawny women and skirt-clinging, underfed children. Life had dealt most of the people so many blows, and they had seen so many itinerants pass through over the years, that even

Jago (if indeed they realized who he was) and his riders, scarcely raised an eyebrow. When you were all the way down, what else was there that could hurt you?

Near an empty corral on the northern limits of Sturrock, Frank Jago, narrow-chested and with thinning, gingery hair, pressed fingers into the small of his back. Long rides now took more out of him than once they had done, and the halts that he had called on this one had grown more frequent as time had gone on. It was now four days since they had burned Ed Maidment.

'The real hard ones,' Jago had said on that occasion, 'they don't wanna yell. But fire, in the finish, it'll break all on 'em.' And he had set out to demonstrate his contention, using a length of dry hardwood that he had picked up behind one of the outbuildings while Maidment was being lashed to a tree and a fire had been set only a few feet away. Even so, it had taken Jago some forty minutes to break

Maidment and during that time it had seemed that the leather thongs the man had been bound with must surely cut through his wrists before he gave way, finally emitting such a scream as to flush birds aloft. At that point, Jago, although himself badly affected through breathing in smoke, had laughed in his triumph, and with the smoking firestick had then blinded Maidment.

Now, to the querulous Culpepper, he said, 'Conrad? Nope. I dunno where. But movin' an' listening an' watchin', that's what's gonna take us to Bob Conrad.' Jago was still wheezing slightly, even now, from the effects of the smoke. 'Don't worry, Cul, I'll sniff out that bastard. I found them others, one by one.' His lips pulled back from his stained teeth. 'How long yuh reckon ol' Bob'll stand the firestick? Longer'n the other 'un?'

Nobody was prepared to guess.

★ ★ ★

In Warbonnet they could have done without Arn Lazlo, past his prime or not. Conrad sure could have done without him. There had been a falling out over cards in a room above a barbershop, and two of the four players there had had to move fast to get Lazlo's arms pinned. Ruddy-faced, white haired, he had cussed them loud enough to be heard in the barbershop below. They had had the good sense to take the Colt Lightning from him before bundling him awkwardly down the bare wood stairs and into the street.

In his day he had been a hard man, arguably still was, and in liquor, a man who could not be reasoned with. It could have been assumed that advancing age had soured him more than somewhat. Shorn of his Colt pistol and of the rifle, scabbarded on his horse at a tie-rail, Arn Lazlo swore that by sundown he would have armed himself and by God he would be back, and the four-flusher he had claimed had carried a sleevecard would turn out to be the biggest loser on the day. Ageing or not, Lazlo, in this mood, was a man who had to be minded.

Conrad was sent for. Before he got there, however, a newspaperman and a photographer who had been stopping over in Warbonnet, on their way back north, got a whiff of an unexpected story that was out of the general run, so followed up on it. When Conrad did arrive he waved the gathering crowd to a healthier distance. He would have fronted Arn Lazlo but by that time the man was nowhere to be seen. Conrad took charge of Lazlo's firearms, unhitched the roan from the barbershop tie-rail and led it along the street and hitched it outside the county jail. There was always the chance that its aggrieved owner would wind up inside the same building before the day was out. Then, having left the weapons at the jail, Conrad set out to locate Arn Lazlo. The newspapermen would have followed him around but Conrad waved them away as he had the crowd outside the barbershop. Even so, in moving further off, the photographer, quietly setting up his tripod, did let go one magnesium flash which froze in time, on the principal street of Warbonnet, the famous Bob Conrad, now a town marshal, fiercely moustached, darkly clad, glancing back with some annoyance at the persistent men from some unknown newspaper, and with whom he might have a word or two later. Marshal in a clapped-out town nobody had heard of he might well be, but as those two knew, the legend still clung to his name, as a different kind of notoriety clung to Arn Lazlo.

It transpired that Lazlo did manage to re-arm himself. He lifted a Walker Colt from a dozing drunk in back of a saloon, and by chance, Conrad, having been searching elsewhere at the time, but coming back onto the main street, saw the white-headed man approaching the barbershop and carrying the pistol.

'Hold up there, Arn . . . !'

Lazlo halted, his flushed face turning towards the marshal. If he was dismayed by the sudden appearance of Conrad, whom he recognized, he did not show it. 'I got no quarrel with you, Conrad.'

'On this street, with a drawn pistol, you have,' Conrad said.

Wherever Lazlo had been in the weeks, and more, before riding into Warbonnet, he had acquired at least some of the news that had been gaining currency elsewhere. Perhaps to unsettle the tall man who had accosted him, he said, 'Didn't reckon to find yuh in a place like this'n, Conrad. What happened to Dave Dryden git to yuh? That what it was?'

Conrad's attention was certainly seized. 'What about Dave Dryden?'

Lazlo, foxy-eyed, showed his ravaged teeth in a grin. 'Don't tell me yuh dunno Dave got his lamp blowed out by Frank Jago?'

The remark must have convinced the white-haired man that Conrad had momentarily been put off balance, and because he had the advantage of a pistol already in hand, within the next twenty seconds Arn Lazlo provided several newspapers with stark evidence that at least part of the west was still what their editors liked to refer to as wild.

To his credit, the photographer, even with his cumbersome equipment, had managed to capture the moment of Conrad's smoky firing, and Lazlo, pistol swung wide of his body, his head thrown back being shot and in the very act of falling backwards. And in a second picture, men coming out on the street, the body of Lazlo sprawled on its back, pistol still clenched in the outflung right hand, the large, somewhat vulturine figure of Conrad nearby, looking down.

* * *

If any demonstration had been needed, the shooting of Arn Lazlo by the town marshal of Warbonnet had served to revive in many minds that they had in their employ a man whose dangerous powers had by no means diminished, and this, no matter what, privately, Conrad himself might believe to be the case.

For Conrad, too, what Lazlo had said, even if only to unsettle him, had come as a shock and had raised all kinds of questions in his mind, not least of which was whether or not the story was true. If it was, then where, and how it had come about was the next question. It was what Conrad had come to look upon as a half story, sometimes only the product of speculation and rumour. Not a lot of news from the outside world came quickly to Warbonnet, even though the railroad passed through. The trains were by no means frequent and for the most part, were freights. There were itinerants, of course, and drummers of one sort or another. The steam-hissing locomotives took on water, and through-travellers stretched cramped legs at the unprepossessing depot, many not venturing even as far as the main street.

The days and weeks went sliding by and a peacefulness descended on Warbonnet. Conrad was given a wide berth, generally, and this was to his liking. Then, early one evening, when he was lying, dozing, on top of his cot, fully dressed apart from his boots, having earlier been half-awakened by the mournful sound of a train whistle, he came fully alert to a tapping at his door. This was in a musty, run-down hotel to which he had moved after Emmie's departure.

'Mr Conrad? Mr Conrad, there's a lady down in the lobby wants to see you . . . '

Conrad, answering, swung his long legs to the floor and groped around for his boots. Another pale, beleagured woman seeking intervention by the marshal, protection, like as not, from yet another workless but unaccountably drunken sot who was knocking her around. Despair and drink. And a lashing-out. No one else to turn to but the marshal. Conrad's powerful appearance might indeed be sufficient to put a stop to it. But a man had come a long way down, to this. Before taking his rest, Conrad had shucked pistol and shellbelt, and now, having reached for them, hesitated, then did not trouble to put them on.

She must have heard him coming down the stairs to the poorly-lit lobby and had then seen the tall, bulky loom of him on the lower landing. Mostly in shadow and wearing a dark, hooded cape, breathing deeply, she was holding the pistol extended before her in both of her gloved hands. If at the very last instant, Conrad saw what was coming, he gave no sign and uttered no word.

The flash and concussion and burst of smoke from the pistol were like a hard-slamming door in the confines of the lobby, and Conrad was spun partly around as he was hit, struck the old, stained wallpaper, then came tumbling noisily down the remaining stairs to fall on the floor of the lobby, the woman still pointing the pistol at where he had been on the landing.

Men came in a rush, the clerk, a couple of others from the recesses of the grubby establishment. She made no effort to resist them as they closed around her, taking the pistol, hustling her to one side away from the fallen Conrad. There was blood on him and on the floor.

'My God! Yuh killed the marshal . . . !'

9

How Kyle, the barber, working under a single lamp, as often as not standing in his own light, could see what he was doing was remarkable in itself. That on the third attempt, Conrad stripped to the waist, lying face down on a long trestle table, Kyle got the .38 lead in the grip of his bloodied forceps, was even more so.

Gripping the top edge of the varnished wood, Conrad was running slickly with sweat, his teeth clenched, having throughout the operation implacably refused to be drugged. He was breathing very hard, his forehead pressed down on the table as he heard the lead ball drop into a tin dish.

'Out!' said Kyle triumphantly.

Breath was hissing between Conrad's teeth, his limbs were quivering and although he badly wanted to get off the table he knew that to do so immediately would result in his not being capable of standing. And he had suffered enough without that additional humiliation. When he could trust himself to speak, however, he asked, 'Where is she?'

'Down in the jailhouse,' the barber said. He was sweating almost as profusely as was Conrad. Now the big man did make an effort to get off the table but the barber advised him to stay right where he was. Conrad gasped as the barber then began sponging all around the wound in his side with sharp-smelling alcohol, then after a pause, placed a gauze-wrapped cloth smeared with salve across the wound itself.

'Stuck out like a thumb, that ball, right close to the left ribs. Coulda hit bone.' It sure had hit something, for Conrad was in acute pain. The barber then produced long strips of plain white cotton cloth and a roll of gauze bandage, and grunting and breathing audibly through his nose, and occasionally saying, 'Lift,' bound the cloths securely into place. Only then did he assist Conrad off the table. The big man swayed but by a major effort of will managed to remain upright. The barber helped him on with his holed and blood-smeared shirt, then his ruptured vest, which Conrad slowly but single-mindedly buttoned. The barber was prepared to bet he would not get ten paces, but Conrad, though sweat-drenched and his face the colour of lard, making his dark moustaches seem even more prominent, ignored him.

The hound-faced Styles was on his own in the dimly-lit county office when, very slowly, Conrad came in, and the lawman's eyes went wide, as though he might have believed that a corpse had arrived.

'Jesus, Bob, you look like shit.'

Propping one large hand on a straight-backed chair, Conrad asked Styles the same thing that he had asked the barber. 'Where is she?'

'Down yonder. Christ, she damn' near done fer yuh. Who the hell is she? Where's she from? She flat out won't talk to me.' A not unreasonable option, Conrad thought. She would have detested Styles on sight.

'She'll talk to me,' he said, and added, 'Alone.'

Styles stood blinking at the very sick-looking marshal and made a gesture towards a bunch of keys on a ring lying on his cluttered desk. Conrad shook his head. So he went on through the office and down a dim passageway, only the light from the office spilling along it, Conrad's enlarged shadow lurching ahead of him.

She was the sole occupant of the county jail and she was on her feet when Conrad arrived outside the bars. She was still wearing her dark-coloured cloak but the hood had been allowed to fall back, revealing, even in this gloom, the glossy sheen of her black hair. There was a bucket in the cell, and judging by the stench, Conrad assumed that she must have vomited into it.

For a few seconds they stood facing one another, the long bars of the cell ribbed between them. Finally, in a low voice, she said, 'I'll always regret not doing it properly.'

'I've known people who fancied themselves at it, miss altogether,' Conrad said. Then, 'Why, Ruth?'

He got all of his history then, according to Ruth Corde, his self-centredness, his basking in the adulation accruing to the Conrad Posse, his taking undue credit for the work of others, his mistreatment of Emmie Naver (Conrad's brow furrowed at that), his abandonment of men he had relied upon when it suited *him*, exposing them and theirs to scum like Frank Jago.

'Dave Dryden, dead.' The words came out like bullets.

'I did hear that.'

'Dead. Shot down on the steps of a church, on his wedding day. Shot like a rabid dog.'

'Where, and when?'

She ignored his questions. 'Sam, dead. Sam, poor fool, tried to take on five men.' She was speaking very quickly now, in almost breathless haste, her voice low. Conrad thought that her eyes were closed but it was by no means easy to tell. 'So he was trying to get across the yard . . . get to the house . . . they had me in the house . . . he got part of the way, but there were others outside and they killed him there . . . one of the great Conrad Posse. On his own, trying to get to the house . . . to me.' Her voice had risen. 'They had me in there, Conrad, and they . . . used me to bring him in . . . In the finish, five men altogether . . . It was *four hours* before they'd done with me! Could you possibly imagine what that was *like*?'

'Ruth . . . !'

'Why they didn't put a bullet in me, too, when they'd finished, I'll never know. Maybe they knew that it would be so much *worse* if they left me alive . . . '

Again, but in a lower tone, he said, 'Ruth . . . '

'So you didn't know about Sam. Tell me something else you didn't know, Conrad. Ed Maidment, dead. And Laura, God knows where.'

'*Maidment?*' Conrad's brain was whirling for he was unable to take all this in. 'Laura . . . '

'Oh yes. Laura. That's getting to the truth of it, Conrad, isn't it? She matters above everybody.'

Conrad, his left side afire, his body sweating, yet chilled, put one hand on the wall, turning half away from the cell. Dryden, Corde, Maidment, all gone. It did not seem possible. Licking dry, cracked lips, he said, 'I'm going to get you released from here.'

'The very last thing I'd want is your charity! I wanted you dead, too, Conrad, like them. So now here I am. I failed. Attempted murder of a town marshal.'

136

'I'll see you get out.' When she said nothing more, Conrad straightened away from the wall and made his painful, uncertain way back up to the office where Styles was. Styles must have heard just about everything, for he now regarded Conrad warily but also sourly.

'I let her out, she could try it ag'in.'

'I'll take my chances.' Stiffly Conrad reached to the desk and picked up the bunch of keys and tossed them to Styles. 'Let her out.' He took out a wallet and from it some bills and dropped them on the desk. 'Get her a room at Bradshaw's. Don't tell her I paid. Then put her on the next train through. Two days.'

Styles stood blinking at the bills on the desk. Presumably he had taken in what Conrad had said to him, but in a low-pitched voice, said, 'There's gonna be hell to pay when it gits known that Frank Jago's on the loose an' might come here.' And, apparently thinking of the Conrad Posse, as much of it as he had picked up, years ago, 'Christ! All dead.' The indestructible destroyed, one by one.

It had been hammering at Conrad too. And he could read, in Styles' expression, the half-accusatory fear that had now aligned itself with Conrad's very presence in Warbonnet. This was the man, once lauded, who had been reduced to throwing drunks out of saloons in a town that most people would never have heard of. None the less, a man it would be strongly advised to walk around with care. Conrad, for all his fall in fortunes, must never be taken cheaply. Take the sudden flare-up with the half drunk one-time pistolman, Arn Lazlo. If it had not been for Conrad's immediate and unswerving intervention, that could have had very bad consequences. Brutal and unsavoury as some might have viewed it, once it was over, the marshal had dealt with it like a skilled dentist pulling a rotten tooth. It would have promoted, on the other hand, because of the accidental presence of newspapermen, wide publicity. Maybe that was exactly what had brought this woman here. And by God, she might well have killed the man. So, if Jago had not known, already, where Conrad was to be found, it was highly probable that he would do now. From the problem of the woman, Styles now faced the prospect of worse events to come.

To Conrad, moving slowly through the night, Ord Jago's words came back. *'Yuh'll never take another step without lookin' to see who's behind yuh . . .'*

For the next few days the town was humming with the story of how Bob Conrad had been shot by a woman, and not just any woman, certainly not some drunken whore, but Ruth Corde, widow of a member of that Conrad Posse. What deep waters might be running there could only be speculated upon. As for Conrad, he had seemingly gone to ground, for since that night he had not been observed making his customary rounds. Two days after the shooting, the county sheriff had been seen escorting a slim, very dark-haired woman to the Warbonnet depot, there to see her aboard the train for San Raphael and points east. But why she had been released without being charged seemed now to be of less consequence than the near certainty that Frank Jago, along with other men, would soon enough arrive in town seeking Bob Conrad, a man who had changed in recent days from being a somewhat comforting asset to a wounded, incapable liability. '*We don't want that Frank Jago findin' him here.*' That was the clear, insistent message that was coming to Styles and was gaining currency throughout the town. A couple of days on, word came in that Jago had been seen at the settlement near Fort Cobb. Still some way from Warbonnet, but, it was argued, why would he be around Ford Cobb if he did not intend coming in this direction? What had been uneasiness became shifty-eyed fear.

10

As day followed day the more weight tended to come on the county sheriff, Styles, about what was now thought to be the certainty that the town of Warbonnet would soon become a killing ground. Of Conrad, during this time, there had been little sign. Then the marshal got his second visitor and almost as great a shock as he had when suddenly confronted by Ruth Corde.

'Laura . . . !'

'At the depot I got a strange reaction when I asked where I could find you.' Then, 'Bob, you look awful . . . '

Stiffly he waved a hand to a chair, then he sat on the edge of the cot and told her about Ruth Corde and what had happened, and saw the shock in her face. Then, 'It was Ruth told me about Ed, and about Sam and Dave. Laura, I'm truly sorry. Ed didn't deserve that. None of them did.'

'Ed had been almost crippled. Almost two years ago, he took a bad fall.' Though clearly tired from her journey she had been holding up well, but now her head went down, and Conrad, rising, could see that she had begun sobbing. He went to her and placed his large hands on her shoulders and waited like that until she could bring herself under control, remembering that he had often thought, in the past, that she always seemed to be so much *in* control. She was dabbing a white cambric handkerchief to her eyes, and in a voice that was husky after tears, she said, 'Bob, you couldn't imagine what they'd done to him . . . burned his eyes out . . . ' She must have felt the grip of his fingers tighten slightly. 'When I came back and found him . . . '

'You weren't there?'

'I was in the town. Stoller. I didn't see Frank Jago, but I heard that Culpepper was there. It must have been after they'd been to the farm. Where

Jago was at the time, I don't know.'
There was another shuddery intake of
breath. 'But you . . . Ruth . . . '

'In Ruth's mind, what happened to
Sam and to her, and to the others, for
that matter, is somehow all down to
me. Maybe she saw something more
between me and the Jagos. The hanging
of Ord. That it had been in my hands
to avoid that, to avoid what's started
this. It wasn't. I couldn't have done
anything about that. He was a man
that sentence had been passed on by
a court, but who'd got away, dodged
the rope. We caught him and took him
back. But Ruth, she was 'way past
that kind of reasoning. Laura, I know
that what happened to her was foul,
terrible, enough to break any woman's
mind. I don't know how she survived
it. Maybe Ruth had to make *somebody*
pay for that.'

Laura, her eyes reddened, looking
directly at him, shook her head. 'I'm
sure it goes much deeper than that.
I mean, it's much more personal than

that, Bob. In the old days, when things were . . . different, every look, every word of hers, when you were there, was plain enough for another woman to read.'

Conrad knew that there would be no use his denying it. The night at the Shafto House Hotel in Daverne came back to him, his rejection of Ruth Corde and the final, malevolent glance that she had reserved for him. Conrad did not pursue it now, but told Laura about Emmie Naver. 'She went off with him, or to meet up with him, in Hainsville. We'd lived in Hainsville before we came here. I found it hard to believe, what she'd done, even though we'd been having problems for some while. I've found out, since, that there were others, other men, going 'way back.'

Laura's lashes came down. Maybe, he thought, she knew more of that, too, than she would be prepared to admit. It could serve no purpose, anyway. Looking up, she said, 'Hainsville. I sent a telegram there, to find you. It was to tell you about Ed and about Dave and Sam, because of the word that had come to us about them. We knew we had no defence any more, but Ed was too proud to ask for help. I went right against his wishes and sent you a message without telling him.'

'Before Ruth came, I'd heard a half tale about Dave. But no telegram got to me. I wish to God it had.'

'It would have been too late to help Ed.' She had been studying his face. 'Hainsville . . . Do you think it possible that Emmie . . . ?'

'I don't know, Laura. Maybe. She was well known there. But we'll likely never know.' He did know, though, was as certain as ever he could be, and a raw resentment rose up in him. Then he said, 'All of us, all of us that were in the posse . . . ' He broke off and in an almost angry tone, said, 'Even the damn' *name* was wrong! It was no posse. We were bountymen. All of us dragged Frank Jago along with us,

146

even when the word was that he'd gone down across the border. I don't know whether he did or not, for a time. But our mistake, my mistake, was in not nailing him. Maybe we all wanted to believe that he had gone, and for good. Maybe that *was* down to me. Giving up. But we'd had enough, Laura. You must have seen that, in Ed.'

'I did.' Again the long lashes came down. 'You say you and Emmie had your bad times, Bob. Ed and I had ours.' She looked up. 'Nothing like . . . what you said about Emmie. What we'd had, if that ever was much, simply . . . died.' As though in an attempt to balance what she had just told him, she said, 'Don't misunderstand me, Bob. I never looked on him as a *bad* man. Never once did he raise a hand to me, never rounded on me with accusations, and he always did his best in what he thought were our interests. It was just . . . we were a wrong pairing. That was as much my mistake as it was his.'

This surprised Conrad and it must

have showed. He said, 'Never once, in all the time I knew him, did he give any hint . . . If . . . ' Conrad stopped abruptly. The large brown eyes were regarding him steadily.

'I can believe that. I said that he wasn't a bad man. He would not have wanted any hint of it to go beyond him and me, to further hurt me. But truly, Bob, we'd come quietly to the end of it. Then the accident happened, and of course, after that I couldn't simply walk away and leave him. It was clear that he knew it, and it gnawed at him. In the end, when he really needed me, I was of no use to him.'

'If you'd been there you'd have had to go through what Ruth went through.'

'And afterwards, not have wanted to go on living.'

'Ruth came through it somehow, and had enough hate left over to share around.'

As he said it she rose from the chair and gently put her small hands on him. 'Go lie on that cot, Bob. Take your shirt off. I want to look at that wound.'

'You've been up here some while. In the house, talk will be starting, I reckon.'

'I don't care about them or their talk. When I'm good and ready I'll go back down and pay for a room.' It was said quietly but firmly. Conrad, obviously in some discomfort, first sitting on the edge of the cot, stripped his shirt off so that the barber's bandage could be unwound. The wound in his left side, soon revealed, was reddened, swollen and very tender, but the salve that the barber had smeared on the folded pad had prevented it from adhering. 'Bob, this badly needs cleansing and dressing again.' Her expression told him that she did not care for the looks of it at all. 'I'm not sure whether or not it's infected.'

'There's no doctor in Warbonnet, and the only druggist is more often drunk than sober. That's why it was the barber that had to probe for the ball.'

'Sit just as you are. I'll go out and get my hands on some clean dressings and some ointment.'

She seemed to have taken a deep breath and recovered herself, perhaps this immediate concern for his needs and the prospect of activity had helped her. A half hour later, he had been cleanly bandaged and was rebuttoning his shirt. Only then did Laura mention to him some men she had seen standing in a group outside the hotel, and who had scrutinized her closely as she went by. 'There were two with badges on their vests, one of them not a young man, the other maybe thirty or so, with a real beak of a nose.'

Styles, the county sheriff, Conrad told her, and one of his deputies, Eckhardt. 'How many others?'

'Eight. Ten, maybe. Some of them were in suits. Merchants, I'd say.'

Conrad nodded. 'The fear's started to bite real hard now. They've made their minds up that Frank's bound to come here for me.'

'It's probably true. He came for Dave and for Sam and Ed. No doubt we all thought that any danger there had been, once, was long past. Ed was sure that whether or not Frank Jago had gone across the border, he'd have died of consumption, anyway.'

Conrad told her that it was a theory that had been sound. 'Ord was in a bad enough way. It was said that, if anything, Frank was worse off. He was out of sight for a long time. Maybe he was resting up.' Out of sight, out of mind. Then Dave Dryden, in a different place, a different world from that of the Conrad Posse, had never known what had hit him. 'This looks to me like Frank's last try to square the book,' Conrad said. 'Frank, he can feel the black angel breathing on his neck. He's not got a lot of time and he's got nothing to lose.'

'So what will you do?'

'I don't want to see him come to Warbonnet and start shooting. It's a dump an' I don't much cotton to the people here, but this mess isn't of their making. Reminds me, some, of Arrowhead, where we took Ord an' where they hanged him. There, they were all on hot coals 'til we climbed on the noon train. When you make a business of what we did, you're seen as kind of contaminated. But I under-estimated Frank. I should have got together some other men, a bigger party and finished what had been started. Ed an' the others had done their share. More. Dave Dryden had a bad arm to show for it. It wasn't all gain.' It had not been all gain with Emmie Naver, either, and he was sure that the outcome of that had been in part because of his long absences. Emmie had never known, either, if he would be coming back to her on a horse or in a pine box in a baggage car. That was the flipside of a coin he had never wanted to look at. A kind of guilt. Realizing that he had not answered her question directly, he said, 'What will I do? I'll quit Warbonnet. I can do it soon an' no regrets. I don't have anything here. Nothing to hold me or even delay me. But you?'

Laura was rolling up unused gauze bandage. 'I sold up what was there. I couldn't go on living in that place. And there was news about you, where you were. All about that man Lazlo.' She seemed uncertain about what to say next, and looked down. When she looked up again she said, 'You can't travel . . . The shape that you're in, you can't go far, Bob, unless you go by train.'

'There's no train for three days,' he said. 'I might not have that long.'

'It would be best to take that chance, and wait.'

He shook his head. 'There was a rumour that Frank had been seen at the settlement near Fort Cobb. If that was true and he's been on the move, since, he could be here well inside three days.'

'I can see that if others are still with

him, you couldn't hope to stand against them.'

'I know it.'

'What about the county lawmen?'

'They want shut of me. You saw 'em, down there.'

'You're not fit enough to ride.'

'There's no other way.'

She had fastened the deep brown eyes on him. 'Then I'll come with you. You can't go alone.'

More than anything he knew that he wanted her to be with him, but he said, 'I can't let you risk being taken by Jago. Wait here an' take the train north, to Lefebre, say. Wait there 'til I come.'

'If you're determined to ride out, you're going to need help. For once, Bob, you won't be able to rely on your strength.'

It was true and he knew that to deny it would be foolhardy. Sourly, he said, 'I've taken lead before, but nothing like this.'

'The instruments the barber used

might not have been clean. And anyway . . . '

She did not go on with the next comment but Conrad reckoned he knew what she had stopped herself from saying.

'And I'm no longer a young man. I know it. My bones tell me. My head tells me, too, but I don't listen.'

'I've got a little money,' Laura said. 'I can buy clothes for riding, a mount and what goes with it. I've not ridden much since Ed and I used to go out along the Pinder, when we were in Auberge. But I'll get by.' Conrad had forgotten that. She seemed the kind of woman who would be too delicate to contemplate riding a long distance.

'It will be a lot harder than the country around Auberge. And getting out of Warbonnet is one thing. Throwing Frank off the scent is another. We'd need a whole lot of luck.' No doubt she would read that as she wished to read it, that he had capitulated over the matter of her going with him.

Laura moved towards the door. 'I've not brought much with me, certainly not much that's going to be of any use, travelling on horseback. But no doubt there are women in Warbonnet who'll be glad of what there is.'

Conrad came gaspingly to his feet. 'I'll come along with you, have a word with Styles on the way.' He took his hat off a peg behind the door. No doubt Laura could see that his mood was bleak. Robert Raines Conrad, no less, about to turn tail and run (as he would see it) and all on account of a malevolent consumptive whose own life might be measured only in months. Weeks, even.

★ ★ ★

They had covered no more than six or seven miles, Conrad on his sturdy black and Laura (wearing a blue shirt and a brown, divided skirt) on a roan, not as good looking an animal as Conrad's but the best that was to be had in Warbonnet at that time. As well as extra canteens they were equipped with capacious pouches, and Conrad had a scabbarded Winchester. Bedrolls were secured behind the cantles. What their intentions were, where exactly they were heading, were matters that Conrad confided to no one, and it had been a quiet, almost resentful knot of men, standing outside one of the stores with the aproned storekeeper who had witnessed the departure of the once-lauded manhunter and the delicate-looking woman who (or so it appeared) would scarcely possess the ability or strength to control the roan horse she was mounted on. In her riding clothes and her shallow-crowned hat with a Spanish brim, she looked like no more than a child alongside the big man mounted on the black.

Conrad had no doubt at all that, beyond the group standing outside the store, the eyes of others would have been fastened on his back as he rode slowly out, observing the direction he was taking, making assumptions about where he and the small, attractive woman were heading. Clearly the Warbonnet peace officers and the townsmen who had been on hand at the time had not known what the hell to make of Laura Maidment. That a man with the reputation of Conrad had been shot by one woman with a connection to the Conrad Posse (and incomprehensibly had been allowed to walk free) and quite obviously had been given comfort by another, had been something beyond the comprehension of those who had been more or less witness to both events. Well, Conrad was the last of those particular bountymen and clearly had lost all of the power that the Posse, so called, had afforded him, so that, far from being an asset to Warbonnet, he had quickly become a liability. Any man whose presence might draw the attention of someone like the terrible Frank Jago was no better than an unburied corpse, attracting flies.

Now Conrad felt that he had to get down and take a rest. It was, he knew, much too soon. A bad start. Laura glanced across at him anxiously.

11

They could hear the stream running, the picketed horses moving and snuffling, but nothing else. The fire was still flickering and Conrad fed it a few more scraps of dry brush. Their meal was over, water had been heated and the tin plates and mugs washed.

Overhead, in a partly cloud-screened sky, a half-shadowed moon had risen. Conrad had been far from content with the distance they had travelled, but that had been due, in the main, to his own inability to push the horse along, for he was still in pain and was sweating profusely. None the less, he was also aware that Laura had been vastly relieved to get down out of the saddle and make this camp. But Conrad said, 'Tomorrow we'll need to make better time. I want to get as far as Monroe.'

'Does a railroad go through there?'

'No. Saulville or Pinto Springs. The nearest town to Monroe would be March.' His head went down and he took a long breath in.

'You'd be best advised to let me take another look at that wound, Bob.'

Conrad did not argue against that, and Laura, by the brightening firelight, leaned close and examined the puffy area all around the hole in his side. 'It's been bleeding again. I think that's not a bad sign. I'll clean it and dress it and maybe by tomorrow you won't be in so much pain. But you shouldn't be riding at all.'

When she had finished the task he did feel less discomfort. Watching her as she rolled up unused bandage and put it inside an oiled silk satchel along with the brown jar of ointment, and tossed the soiled bandage on the fire, he was moved to marvel at the way in which, in spite of cramp, she had managed to endure this, for her, unaccustomed way of travelling. For how long she would be able to keep it up was quite another matter. Yet the way in which she had virtually taken over at the camp, gathering dry brush, making a fire, cooking a meal and brewing up coffee, then cleaning up afterwards, all this in spite of the aching weariness she must be feeling, had astonished him and drawn his admiration. He thought it best, now, to level with her about his plan for this journey, even though carrying it out would test him to the utmost, and must surely be daunting for Laura. So he returned to the answer that he had given her earlier.

'The nearest town from Monroe would be March. It's in almost a direct line, north-east.' He paused. 'That would be the obvious way to go, even though there's no railroad going through there. If Frank does get on our trail he'll damn' soon work that out. So, a couple of miles on the other side of Monroe, we'll cut south-east to the foot of the Caine Range. I have to say it's not easy country, an' going that way, taking a wide swing, will take us longer, take more out of us. But if we go the more direct way there's a good chance that Frank, if he's coming, will run us down. Doing it my way, nobody in Monroe would be able to pass on to Frank the direction we've really taken. They'd assume we were on our way to March. And there's one more thing. If Frank thinks he's closing on us, he'll want to press on with it, an' that could cost *him*. He's a sick man.' The irony of what he had just said struck him and he gave the woman a wry grin. 'There's a few about. You might yet live to regret coming with me, Laura.'

'No, I'll not regret it.' Conrad could not see her face clearly now, for she was looking down, not directly at the fire. He extended a hand and found that without hesitation her silky fingers slipped into it. 'We'll come through this, Bob. That doesn't mean that I'm not mortally afraid of Frank Jago and his stray dogs. I saw what they'd done to Ed. You know how strong Ed was, in his good years. Probably you know it better than I do. Well, they must have *broken* him. They could simply have shot him the way they did Dave and Sam. He was defenceless. But they tied him to a tree and . . . did all those things to him, for how long, God knows. They might have kept him living and *feeling* for hours. I've thought about it and thought about it. It would have been easy for them to have waited for me to come back. If they had looked around the house they must have known that there was a woman living there, even if they hadn't known it before. But they didn't wait. They let me go back and find him. Maybe they thought I'd try to warn *you* and if I did, they were . . . sending you a message about . . . what you can expect.' Her small hand tightened its hold on his. 'But that doesn't change anything, Bob. It's my choice. I know where I want to be.'

Conrad went on looking at her. There could be no doubt, now, that their relationship had moved to another level. The gravity of their present circumstances had hastened what might have been inevitable.

★ ★ ★

For some while they had been within sight of the bluish smear of smoke that marked the town of Monroe. So far Conrad had been riding more easily, but had not increased the pace to any great extent. It would be nearer to noon than to mid-morning when they rode in.

Away across to their right, over undulating country, rose the purplish shapes of the Caines, and it was towards that much more broken and hence much more testing country that they would go when they had passed a few miles beyond Monroe. The sharp lift of that town's false fronts was now clear against the partly-clouded sky; not a large town, and by Conrad's account (for he had passed through it a couple of times, some good while back) no more appealing to the eye than Warbonnet.

Between last night's camp and now, they had seen no one, even at a distance, nor had they passed anyone, so that it had seemed that they were lone travellers through an almost silent land. The horses were now being kept down to a walk, Conrad's eyes probing everywhere as they approached one end of what was a wide main street flanked by the usual assortment of structures, the principal one of which was a general store. A few people were about, men for the most part, and it was as they came abreast of a poled corral at the top end of the street that there appeared to be some interest occasioned by their approach. Someone called something indistinguishable, and a couple of men went indoors. As Conrad and Laura were coming by a feed store, a man holding a shotgun stepped out and wagged the long twin barrels.

'Whoo up there, mister . . . '

Conrad and Laura Maidment drew rein.

The man stepped down off the boardwalk. Squarely built, he was wearing moleskin pants and a grey woollen shirt with wide brown galluses over it, and he wore a hat that was very stained around the lower crown. Conrad's eyes held the other man's for a few seconds, then looked across to the right as he heard the sound of a rifle being levered. A second man, this one wearing a black apron almost covering all of his pants and shirt, was standing at the mouth of an alley holding a Winchester.

The shotgunner, a man with a husky voice, asked, 'Your handle Conrad?'

Barely perceptibly, Conrad nodded.

'Then what yuh got to do, Conrad, is keep movin'.'

'What's the problem here?'

'I ain't got one. Arch, over yonder, he ain't got one neither. We aim to keep it that way. The word we got is Frank Jago, he's got a big problem an' it turns out it's you. Now Frank, he come through here a while back, so we know all about the bastard. He ain't gonna give up on yuh, Conrad. He won't be forgivin' of them that gives yuh any help. In that kind o' humour, Frank cain't be handled. Now, you're the bait that'll fetch him an' his boys here.' The shotgunner's eyes flicked to Laura, tarried for several seconds before returning to Conrad.

'We're not asking for a lot,' Conrad said. 'Somewhere to get a meal, a spell for the animals.'

'Yuh don't hear so good,' the shotgunner said.

Conrad felt rather than saw that the man in the apron had brought the butt-plate of the Winchester to his shoulder. From another building further along the street, where several horses were hitched to a tie-rail, three other men had emerged and were watching what was going on. They had pistols stuck in the waistband of their pants. Finally Conrad said, 'You make a good argument, friend. We'll trouble you no more.' He glanced to Laura who, throughout, though clearly tense, had made no move and had uttered no sound. Wordlessly, still, she walked the roan horse around at Conrad's small signal, headed away, Conrad bobbing along in her wake, in a direction which, after they had gone, might lead the men in Monroe to conclude, '*March. They rode on, an' it was towards March.*'

Coming up alongside Laura, casting an eye upwards, Conrad smiled sourly. 'Words are flying ahead of us. On the damn' wire.'

'Then it will fly ahead of us again.'

'Yeah, I reckon so. To March. But in that town, they'll wait a hell of a long time to no purpose.' As they rode on, from time to time Conrad half turned (but stiffly) to regard the country behind them, and the diminishing shapes of Monroe. Once, he remarked, 'Nobody coming to see us on our way.' When later, they stopped and both looked back, even the smoke

169

that had been hanging above the town was no longer visible. 'Just to be sure we're on our own,' said Conrad, 'we'll go another three, four miles before we turn towards the Caines.' The affair in Monroe was still niggling at him and he reflected that this sure was a time when old fears and jealousies were coming to the surface, the wounded or hurt animal set upon by its own kind.

They made their change of direction after dismounting to stretch cramped limbs, and drank from canteens. They had encountered a small rain shower, but the air was humid, the sparse raindrops warm, but Conrad had pointed to the towers of cloud riding over the shadowy peaks ahead of them.

Laura nodded. 'A storm coming?'

'Looks like it. If it heads this way, maybe it'll last long enough to wash out any tracks. I don't know how good Frank is on tracks.'

After a short pause, she said, 'I know his brother was hanged, but men have been hanged before without setting off something like this.'

'It's the one thing left in his life. Every time Frank looks down he sees the grave. Money's no use to him. Possessions. This is all there is left.'

'Do you think the other men will still be with him?'

'I have to assume so. James Culpepper, he's a real bad man, but he's somewhat short on wits. For years, he's leaned on Frank. Probably won't know what to do, once Frank's gone. Ed Harries, he's another that's been around the Jagos for so long that maybe he doesn't know how to do anything else. And there are others that come an' go. So there could still be a party of five. Ruth said five.'

'You don't seem to be bitter about what went on in Warbonnet. Or Monroe.'

Conrad, shifting slightly in the saddle for greater comfort, smiled, but it was more like a grimace. 'After a while you learn not to put too much faith in people.'

'When the Posse was in full cry it was a different song they were all singing, in towns just like those.'

Conrad gave her a sidelong glance. 'Touch of bitterness there, Laura.'

What she might have said was never to be known, for Conrad, staring ahead again, muttered something and wagged one hand urgently as a signal to halt.

'What . . . ?'

'Look, there.' He was pointing towards the sharp profile of the Caines. As the two of them, their mounts jerking heads, stared into the distance, there could be no doubt about what Conrad had seen. Along their line-of-ride, dust was rising, enough of it to be coming from numerous riders, riders coming towards them, and by the looks of it, not wasting time about it.

12

There was no point in their trying to turn and run. Even if the horses were up to it, neither Conrad in his weakened state nor Laura with her limited experience of handling a strong horse would have been able to make a sustained ride.

Conrad said, 'Get ready to dismount fast if we have to. If it's them, we'll just have to stand and fight.' He ignored the quick, alarmed look as he unscabbarded the Winchester and levered a round into the chamber. Though watching the growing dust-cloud and the now distinguishable horses, from time to time she flicked a glance at Conrad's hard, implacable face, and it was possible, she thought, that she was looking at a face that others had seen, years ago, as the Conrad Posse had been going about its hazardous and bloody business. This was an almost alarmingly different Conrad.

Yet suddenly his attitude altered, appearing to relax a little, the butt-plate of the rifle being rested on a knee and he nodded towards the oncoming horsemen.

'There's a guidon flying. U.S. Cavalry.'

The tension began draining out of Laura, too, and she gripped the saddlehorn with one hand, lest she lose her balance, such was the sensation of weakness sweeping through her.

When the approaching detachment — which appeared to comprise about a dozen men, one riding out ahead — was about fifty yards away there came the sound of a short, yapping command and there was a raising of a gloved hand from the man leading. The entire body of horsemen came bobbing down to a halt some fifteen yards away, more dust rising and drifting away. The officer, in his black felt hat, and who had been leading, walked his horse forward and gave them a casual salute, looking very hard at Laura in her Spanish-brimmed hat.

'Lieutenant Eugene Bridges, Fifth Cavalry, Fort Brader.'

Conrad nodded. 'Bob Conrad.' His head turned slightly. 'Mrs Maidment.' When Bridges continued staring at them out of his red-rimmed eyes set in a narrow face that was crusted with dust and running with sweat, Conrad enquired, 'What brings the Fort Brader cavalry this far south-west?'

'Six wild bucks out of the Lebon Creek reservation. Got hold of whiskey, some weapons, daubed on the war paint. Shot a cowman and stole some horses. I take it you've seen no sign of them, Mr Conrad?'

'No.'

'And you've come from where?'

Conrad was in a cleft stick. He had no desire to appear obtuse, yet at the same time wanted to conceal details of what had occurred in the recent past, particularly in Monroe. This young man, with his own problems, anyway, might well dismiss as bizarre some yarn about a wild bunch with an axe to grind, presenting a lethal threat to a man and woman who were, for reasons not given, travelling through undeniably inhospitable country. Finally Conrad said, 'Warbonnet.'

The lieutenant, steadying his muscle-moving, head-shaking horse, must have thought that there was something about Conrad which suggested that it would be pointless asking further questions. Bridges had in fact had a long and so far unsuccessful search which, in all likelihood, he had not chosen to carry out.

Finally Bridges said, 'I can't tell you what to do, but my advice is to keep a close eye on your horses, especially at night.'

'Forewarned,' Conrad said, 'is fore-armed.' He suspected that this man was now beyond the limits of his knowledge and his patience, so that the probability of his finding the group that he sought was becoming less likely by the day. Behind him a sergeant and twelve troopers waited on their sweat-rimed, dusty horses. The guidon, on a lance, hung limply.

They parted company, Bridges stiff-waving his detachment on, curious eyes raking the man and woman unexpectedly encountered in this unappealing place as the troopers went bobbing by. Conrad, watching their departure, was pensive. Fourteen pairs of eyes were heading along what was Conrad's back-trail. The thought unsettled him, but there was nothing he could do about it.

As they drew nearer to the Caines, the peaks rearing above them, dwarfing the riders, the bulging grey clouds were bending far over the tops. Conrad pointed towards a gap between two rocky outcrops, for there appeared to be a cave, or at least an overhang beneath which they might shelter until the coming storm should pass.

The way in, between upthrusts of

ancient rock and some patches of scrawny brush, had to be taken at a walk, and then, having gone up a shallow, sandy slope, they came onto virtually level ground. But on either hand were almost sheer rock-faces. The open space between was cluttered with weather-worn boulders which during past ages must have come tumbling from the heights.

The place they sought was indeed a partly boulder-screened cave which they were to discover was some sixty feet in depth, its entrance beneath an overhang of dark granite. There was sufficient clearance to enable them to ride in.

It was a timely arrival, for no sooner had they dismounted than there came a wrenching crack of thunder and a flicker of lightning. While they were still able to do so, they went outside and gathered armsful of tinder-dry brush, took it back and dumped it inside the cave. Conrad then placed some of it near the cave's mouth and soon had a fire crackling. They boiled water for coffee. Even though Conrad was still moving stiffly he was in less discomfort than he had been on the previous day, and Laura seemed more alert and less affected by long spells in the saddle.

But the most obvious change was the way in which they worked together, scarcely needing to exchange words; a glance, a nod, a gesture sufficient for complete understanding. Conrad, in all his life, had never felt more comfortable with anyone, man or woman.

While they were sipping coffee, more thunder bursting in the grey sky, further flashes of lightning occasionally illuminating the dimness of the cave, Laura spoke again about Ed Maidment. 'He was an independent man, to the point of stubbornness, but, did you know, he felt *gratified* that you approached him to become one of that group. So, don't feel guilt, Bob.'

'You can read me better than most,' he said. Then he said what, almost certainly, he would not even have hinted to another living soul. 'This is it, Laura. The last time. When we get to Pinto Springs we'll board the train there, go . . . go anywhere but some other clapped-out cowtown. I've taken my last hit. It's finished.'

She was regarding him with large-eyed seriousness, perhaps a kind of sadness. Very quietly she said, 'I doubt I shall ever shake free of the sight of Ed, how they left him. I've always known that this was a raw country, cruel too, Bob, but I didn't know there was as much naked *hate* as that, in all the world. I've dreamed about it, woken up in a sweat, as though I was *feeling* what he must have gone through.'

Conrad reached across and took one of her small hands. 'He was a good man, Laura. A real hard man, too. There were times, in bad situations, when I've blessed the chance that gave me his friendship. His loyalty.'

'After the accident, he didn't want anyone who'd known him to see how . . . how badly affected he was. He was a proud man, always afraid of being thought stupid. I'm not sure where I stood, with him, at the finish. People can come to resent being *helped*. I truly don't know how he saw me. At times I don't know how I saw myself. Righteous? Doing the *right thing*? Sometimes I felt good about it, sometimes not.'

'You have to try to put it behind you. Nothing can be changed now, Laura.'

Rain came, a heavy thundershower sweeping across the face of the cave, a steady downpour which lasted for almost ten minutes, then dwindled away, the sound of thunder having moved farther off. The rain virtually stopped and the smell of fresh, damp earth and an old decay invaded the cave.

Conrad turned his head sharply, then quickly scooped sand from the floor of the cave and flung it on the fire, smothering it. Somewhere outside, a horse had whickered. The heads of the two horses further back in the cave came up, and ears flicked. Conrad gasping, Laura reaching instinctively to steady him, struggled to his feet and went to the black horse and unshipped the Winchester, then walked to the mouth of the cave. Unasked, Laura visited Conrad's saddlebags and withdrew a red and white waxboard box of ammunition.

'Whoever it is,' Conrad said, 'must have been close enough to see the smoke.' The cavalry detachment? If so, what would have caused them to come back? Someone else? There had been no rise of dust along Conrad's back-trail. Almost at once he got his answer about who it was. A rifle shot fetched a howling ricochet off the granite overhang above the entrance to the cave and at the same time an unholy yell split the air. Conrad said, 'Keep as low as you can, an' come close up to the boulders here. We've got Lieutenant Bridges' Indians.' There came a rushing of horses. Conrad glimpsed them as they went by some fifty yards away, moving in and out between boulders and brush, and read it as a feint. 'Four,' he said. 'I saw just four. Bridges said six. Maybe they're short of horseflesh.'

'They saw us come in here?'

'From a distance, maybe. Made sure the horse-soldiers were well out of the way before they moved in on us.' He had hardly got the words out before one of them, running, came right at him. The Indian was so close and coming so fast that Laura gave a small cry.

This was a wild-eyed youth wearing moccasins, a breech-clout and daubed with red and yellow paint. He was armed with a long cavalry pistol of war vintage, and when Conrad, the Winchester at hip level, shot him in the chest, fired the dated weapon into the air. The charging warrior was stopped by the impact of the .44 lead as though he had run into the side of a barn. Then he lurched to one side as Conrad levered and shot and hit him a second time. The Indian fell only a matter of feet from the entrance to the cave, and alongside one of the screening boulders. Conrad warned Laura, 'Don't stand up.' She was crouching level with his knees.

Yapping like dogs, the mounted Indians were coming back, this time all shooting as they rode. Conrad, crouching over Laura, sheltering behind the boulder, was alarmed lest some of the incoming lead might ricochet inside the cave and strike the horses. And in his mind, there was the unknown whereabouts of the second Indian who was also probably afoot. The whooping horsemen went on by.

The second Indian, painted and dressed like the first, but armed only with a broad-bladed knife, came over the top of the smooth boulders like a quick lizard and it was all that Conrad could do to avoid being smothered. Yet he jerked the muzzle of the rifle upwards, catching the brave in the

184

mouth and snapping his head back. But Conrad went staggering backwards too, and fell. Laura went scampering away to one side, away from them. Face contorted with venom, the breech-clouted Indian raised his knife over Conrad just as Laura flung a handful of sand in his face, so that Conrad was given the instant's reprieve in which to lift the Winchester and fire it. The top of the Indian's head sprayed blood as the .44 ploughed through it, and he was slammed away, fetching up against the boulder. The horsemen were coming back, but this time angling in towards the cave.

Painfully Conrad got to his feet and walked forward. Leaning against the hard stone and seemingly unmindful of incoming fire, he shot calmly, levered, lined up and shot again. When the mounted Indians went peeling away, crouching over the necks of their horses, there were but two of them, two loose horses running with them. All vanished among boulders and brush.

Conrad tried to drag first one, then the other of the dead men outside, but failed, and Laura came to help him. Together they managed to drag both bodies several yards away, then quickly went back inside the cave. Conrad, his face drawn, began feeding fresh loads into the Winchester.

Laura asked, 'Will they have gone?'

'No.' he said. 'They'll wait 'til just after sundown or 'til just before sunup.'

'Then we'll not be able to get out? Could we move tonight?'

He shook his head. 'I'd want to know exactly where they were. I can't let you take the risk of them getting hold of you. They've been hit hard. The horses they wanted won't matter any more. They don't need them. But before they move on, they'll want to see me over a fire. Young bucks. Probably still got liquor. I wouldn't want to try to outguess them, even so.' Slowly he went back down the cave, then soon came back again. 'The horses are fine.' He looked hard at her. 'Best hunker

186

down an' wait. It could be a long day an' a longer night.'

After what seemed only a matter of minutes he was shaking her gently. Fumblingly she got to her feet, whispering, 'What is it?' And, 'What time is it?'

'A couple of hours before sunup.'

Laura could scarcely believe that she had slept for so long. Her head was fuzzy and her limbs felt cramped.

'Probably just as well you did,' Conrad said. Then, 'I reckon they've gone.'

'Gone?'

'They've taken their dead.'

Her hands crept to her face. 'They . . . came as close to us as that?'

'They must have. But I heard not a sound.'

She was suddenly aghast. 'Bob, you've not slept?'

'Dozed. I couldn't risk dropping off.'

'You must be exhausted.' He was, or near to it.

'What I want you to do, Laura, is

take charge of the rifle. I'm going to stretch out an' get some sleep. Lie down behind me at right angles, rest the rifle across me. There's a round ready to fire. Anything moves at the mouth of this cave, pull the trigger.' He unthonged the hammer of the pistol and slid the weapon from its holster, got down and lay with it gripped in his hand. 'Give me four, five hours.'

It was in fact close to noon when she shook him awake. She had left him to sleep longer than he had stipulated, yet even so, he was slow to come to his senses. Laura made no apology but asked if the fire should be lit.

Finally up on his feet, albeit unsteadily, Conrad said, 'I'll go out an' take a look around first, make sure they've gone.' He took the rifle but left the pistol with her, a weapon that she held awkwardly, in both hands.

Conrad ventured outside most cautiously. The sky had now cleared, the sun was strong and there was virtually no evidence of yesterday's downpour. He moved, crouching slightly, from boulder to boulder and from one clump of brush to another, rifle held at hip level. He carried out a wide-ranging search of the secluded area, often glancing behind him or making a complete, slow turn, and sometimes looking up at the high rock walls. It was fifteen minutes or more before he returned to where Laura was.

'No sign. An' they covered their tracks well. A few empty shells is all. We can risk a small fire, make a meal before we pull out of here.' It sounded simple, yet Conrad was an old enough dog to know that in this land, nothing could be taken for granted. And there was still a big stretch of alien country between them and Pinto Springs.

13

The miles were drifting behind them as they rode through undulating country, the ravines and canyons of the Caine Range close at their right hand. The possibility that the two reservation Indians might yet make another attack was still very much alive in Conrad's mind, but he was gambling that, if it should come he would be able to make a fast and effective defence. As he rode he was carrying the Winchester and had ensured that Laura was positioned to his left and level with him, so that she was screened from the most obvious places of possible ambush.

Although they had lost a great deal of time, Conrad was not pushing the animals on at a great pace. He was aware that within a few miles there was a river that emerged from the Caines, the Ondero, and it was there that they would pause to refresh themselves and their horses. Yet he was anxious, and though he had not imparted all of his worries to Laura, he had developed a deep feeling of unease, believing that he could almost *smell* Jago coming.

Yet though he had not confided these concerns to her, Laura, with a strange prescience, had noticed the deepening of his withdrawn mood even as he had spoken confidently of reaching the Ondero within about four hours. If his apparent withholding of confidences had disappointed her, she took care not to show it, content that, in all other ways, their time together had brought about a quiet intimacy whose depth and quality was such that it could have been the outcome of a much longer and closer association. She supposed that in part it was because they had now been through the fire together, and had forged the kind of bond that must have existed between the members of the Conrad Posse. In the cave, Conrad had come very close to a dreadful death, she to weeks, perhaps months of unspeakable treatment if the renegades had taken her and had managed to vanish deep into the Badlands, where risk of their being found would have been slim. Even now, bobbing along beside a sober-faced Conrad, Laura shuddered again at the realization of how close it had really been.

In the course of it all, Laura had surprised herself. This present situation was far from her way of life, and gave rise to other thoughts. How often, for example, she had watched Ed Maidment ride away, heading for unforgiving country, much like this, to face the possibility of a violent death, while she, remote and in comparative safety, simply waited for his return. Yet it was now far too late to be concerned about her possible failure to appreciate fully what had been taking place, what Maidment had been a part of. She glanced across at Conrad riding beside her. Not long before the attack, he had said, '*This is it, Laura. The last time.*'

He had been letting her know that he wanted to break free from the old ways, put himself — and her — well beyond the reach of old hatreds. Her thoughts were interrupted when Conrad reached across and touched her elbow.

Not far ahead of them, where there was a large area of brush, several buzzards were lifting into the sky, the big-winged death-birds circling lazily, perhaps disturbed by the approach of the horses, yet reluctant to leave whatever they had been feasting on. Conrad, as they hauled up, said, 'Wait,' then walked the black horse forward, rifle held in his right hand, pointing it as he would a pistol. Abruptly he stopped the horse again and Laura was surprised when he hauled it around and came back to where she was. Quietly he said, 'Get down an' hold the horse close at the head.'

'What is it?'

'I don't believe the buzzards would have lifted just because we were coming. Something else, closer, did it.' When she gave him a look of alarm, he said, 'The two that got away. We'd see the birds, then come in close to find out what they were feeding on.' Conrad's sweeping stare was taking account of their situation, seeking the best, closest cover. This time they would not get to some cave and he rejected the notion of getting themselves pinned in some ravine at the foot of the Caines. Chances were that they would never be allowed to get that far, anyway. He pointed to some brush, near which was a shallow depression in the ground. 'We'll get down in there. I'll hitch the horses in behind some brush.'

Unquestioningly Laura headed for the place Conrad had chosen, he urging her to keep as low as possible, while he went jogging, leading both horses, towards brush high enough to screen them from view. He did not get them there. A rifle shot lashed out and the horse that Laura had been riding screamed and went down, thrashing,

Conrad being knocked to his knees. The second shot came almost atop of the first, and Conrad's black threw up its head, jerking free of Conrad, and fell heavily. Further rifle shots sent bullets whacking into the horses, Laura's mount dying almost at once. But the black was still alive and in a piteous state. Conrad rolled over, knelt close to its head and shot it, then went scampering sideways, towards Laura.

'Oh, God . . . Bob . . . !'

'Hug the ground . . . There's nothing we can do. The horses are gone.' Lying on one side, Conrad, great strain showing in his face, was levering another round into the chamber. Lead came scorching over the top of them, slashing through brush. 'Just stay still,' Conrad said. A silence fell. The day's heat was increasing and flies were darting around them. It took all of Laura's self control to lie still, her face pressed against one of her bent arms. Ten minutes went by. Fifteen. Conrad seemed not to have moved a muscle, but very quietly he said, 'The buzzards have come down again. That probably means those two warriors have moved. One will be circling left, the other right. Lift your head a bit, watch that side. If you see anything moving, tell me quietly. I'll be watching the other way.' She did not say anything but by now he was confident that she would do exactly as he had asked and, bad as their position was, he was astonished that, not only had she endured the rigours of this journey, but had gone through the terrors of recent hours and had managed to keep her reason. Everything around her, everything that had taken place, was completely alien to her. Perhaps, after the horror of Ed Maidment's end, she believed that nothing else that happened to her could possibly be worse. Conrad was blinking sweat from his eyes. His side was still very stiff but not as painful. A half-hour had gone by.

Laura whispered, 'Why don't they come?'

'They can bide their time. They know we can't go anywhere.' Then, 'Do you need water?'

'Yes, but ... '

Conrad began inching forward along the shallow depression towards the dead horses. The animals were seething with flies. Still moving slowly, Conrad could see one of the canteens and eventually reached towards it. A rifle lashed and even as Conrad whipped his outstretched hand away the canteen jumped with the impact of the bullet. It did not rip free but water came spurting from it. Edging back the way he had come, Conrad was shaken and angry. Laura, at the sound of the shot, must have turned her head. Now she said softly, a catch in her voice, 'That means we're done for ... ' Then, urgently, 'Bob ... !'

Conrad swivelled his head in time to see a breech-clouted, painted figure vanish in behind brush only eighty feet from them. Gasping, Conrad rolled and brought the Winchester to bear.

197

He let go one shot that went crashing dustily through the brush, sending bits flying. Conrad shot again, but it was blind shooting. The Indian could have moved away quickly, unseen. Again a silence fell. Ten minutes dragged by, Laura and Conrad shaking their heads, trying to dislodge persistent flies. Finally, Laura said, 'I can't stand much more of this.'

Awkwardly he slid the pistol towards her. 'Hold it in both hands. Anything moves, let go a shot. You might not hit him but it'll give him something to think about.'

'What are you going to do?'

'Go in at the other bastard, the one that ruptured the canteen.'

'Bob, for God's sake take care . . . '

Conrad rose to his feet, and, crouching, ran towards the brush behind which he reckoned one of them to be. Probably it was foolhardy but he had to force the issue. He did not know how long his strength might hold out and he was certain that Laura was not in good shape.

Sharp arms of brush came whipping at him as he went plunging through, rifle at hip level and suddenly came bursting into a little clearing where the buzzards were, the big-winged birds rising as he arrived. They had been feasting on a dead horse, probably one of those the Indians had been riding, near the cave. Beyond the brush at the opposite end of the clearing he could see dust rising. Conrad lowered the rifle. He began retracing his steps. The Indians had gone and Conrad now realized that it had had nothing to do with him. They had heard something that only now had come to his own ears. Other horsemen were coming. Clearly the Indians had concluded that the cavalry detachment was now on its way back, carrying out yet another sweep, searching for them.

When Conrad reached Laura he said, 'They've gone. We can gather up the other canteens now. And listen . . . '

Her face dust-covered, she raised

her head, her large eyes seeming to be deeply sunk in their sockets, the rims reddened. 'Horses.'

'Lieutenant Bridges.'

They went to the fly-swarming horses and untied two usable canteens, then backed away, out into the open. Conrad was squinting into the heat-haze. The horsemen were taking their time. Then there they were, a bunch of them bobbing along, raising dust. Conrad stared at them. He said, 'Get back out of sight. Back into the brush. Get behind boulders if you can. It's not cavalry. I don't know who they are.'

Laura went, seeking to get out of sight quickly, Conrad following, but it was clear that they had been seen for the oncoming riders had increased their pace and there was what sounded like shouting. Conrad found that Laura had paused in an open space where there were a few small boulders. Better than nothing, but not good cover.

No doubt the approaching riders would have seen the dead horses.

Indeed, Conrad now caught sight of the heads of the party going by in clouds of dust, and his worst fears were confirmed when someone yelled, 'Time's come, Conrad . . . !'

Any shred of hope was thereby swept away. Frank Jago had arrived.

14

After the riders had gone rushing by, having pinpointed where Conrad and Laura had gone to ground, just as had happened with the two Indians, no more was heard for a while. But after maybe six or seven minutes, some shots were heard. Yet no bullets came flying over the two crouching amid the brush. It seemed that the rifles were being fired into the air, a few seconds' interval between each shot, and each one from a different quarter.

'Plain enough,' Conrad said. 'He's letting us know that they're all around us.'

That was all that was heard for fully another five minutes, then a reedy voice called out, 'Too bad about them animals o' yourn, Conrad! 'Nother few minutes an' them redskins woulda fried yuh!' Evidently the Indians were known

202

about, which made Conrad thoughtful.

Another silence fell. Laura, as she had asked about the Indians, now held back from asking, '*Why don't they come?*' She knew why. Unlike the drunken Indians, these men surrounding them fully realized who it was that they had cornered. Bob Conrad, armed, afoot and at bay. Five of them there might well be, but passing through the mind of even the most witless among them would be the knowledge that if all five were to come in at him in a rush, while they would almost certainly overwhelm him, at least two of them would be dead. So, who among them would survive, and who would lie in this Godforsaken place, attracting flies?

Jago's voice came again. 'Thought yuh was . . . ' (here there came the sounds of coughing that went on for maybe half a minute). A pause. More coughing. Silence. Then, 'Thought yuh was free an' clear, I bet . . . you an' (coughing) you an' Maidment's woman . . . too bad yuh run across that boy-soldier . . . '

Sombrely Conrad thought, '*Down our backtrail.*' An unfortunate turn of a card if ever there had been one. But he was listening intently for any sound which would tell him that any of them were on the move, towards him. So far he had heard nothing. But the heat in this place was becoming worse, the flies were numerous and determined, and Laura, in particular, was having trouble keeping still, trying repeatedly to dislodge them from her face. This was part of Jago's plan, to keep them pinned down in rising heat and discomfort, keep them guessing and to do his utmost to goad them into some rash act. When he had managed to draw no response from Conrad, Jago now called out to Laura.

'That man o' yourn, Miz Maidment, turned out he wasn't near as hard as he thought. (A bout of coughing.) Yuh did figure he was a hard man? Let me (a pause, perhaps holding back more coughing) . . . tell yuh, when he broke, he sure broke . . . ' Then, 'Where was yuh, Miz Maidment? In town? (Further coughing, and hawking and spitting.) When we got aroun' . . . to fryin' the bastard's balls, why it sure is a wonder yuh didn't hear 'im . . . all that way to Stoller.'

Conrad saw that she had brought her gloved hands to her ears, shut her eyes and tilted her head down. He reached out and grasped one of her narrow shoulders, then when she looked up, said, 'They could come in, slow an' easy, maybe while he's yapping. If they do, you'd best make a smaller target.' At his gesture she moved back from where she had been crouching.

With the butt of the rifle Conrad, sweat dripping from him, began digging and raking at the sandy ground, and as soon as she saw what he was doing, Laura began helping him, scooping the light, loose soil away with her gloved hands. They worked at it singlemindedly (though Conrad did pause briefly from time to time, to listen) until they had made a trench about six feet in length and twelve or fourteen inches deep. Conrad had wanted it deeper but the effort had cost him, and for almost a minute he had to grasp the rifle tightly by the barrel, butt set firmly on the ground, supporting himself with it. Breathing harshly, he said, 'Lie down in it. Hold on to the pistol. It could make the difference, when they start shooting.' It was makeshift, the price of not having been able to get into better cover.

That was the moment when Conrad, his head coming up and pressing a gloved finger to his lips, heard the first sound other than Jago's high-pitched voice. The men who were with Jago did not have the stalking skills of an Indian. Moving almost silently among rough brush was beyond them. Conrad made pointing signs to the left, Laura, in her prone position lifting her head slightly.

Sixty feet away an upper branch

206

quivered and a twig cracked. Conrad, down on one knee, levelled the Winchester, lining up some four feet below the movement that he had seen. When he thought his eye had caught the merest touch of colour he let go a lashing shot, saw bits of dusty brush go flying, then a man, a thickset individual in a blue shirt, black vest and leather leggings and holding a rifle, rose up, went staggering sideways, losing his hat and falling with a smashing of branches. He had not uttered a sound. Conrad reloaded and waited. Laura's head was down again but she was none the less managing to watch Conrad.

Conrad was listening intently. The sounds where the rifleman had gone down had ceased. Not Jago. Not Culpepper. Not Harries. Though he had seen the man only once before, he thought it could have been Zac Avery. The noise of Conrad's rifle, and the sounds of breaking branches and the small flurry of dust that had been caused, were followed by a further

207

silence. Because the man Conrad had shot had spoken no word and had not cried out it was possible that his companions were as yet unaware of what had happened. Jago, it seemed, did not yet know, for again he called to Laura.

'Miz Maidment . . . ? Yuh hear me . . . ? Soon as we git through burnin' Bob Conrad, which yuh don't wanna miss (a short cough), the boys'll wanta git to the pickin's. Best yuh take what comes 'thout givin' us no trouble . . . Sam Corde's uppity woman, she had a mind to hold out, so she got slapped around some 'til she come to see reason . . .'

Laura lay still, not even bothering about the flies now, as though she had set her mind to ignoring them. She was gripping the now-cocked pistol. She was facing one way, Conrad the other, as they had done after the Indians had killed the horses. There came to them the sound of words being spoken but no sense could be made of what was being said. Conrad muttered that he thought they had at last missed Avery.

Then a medium-sized man wearing torn levis and a brown shirt with black galluses over it, came easing through brush, a pistol lining up on Conrad's back at a range of some fifty feet. Laura, squeezing the quivering pistol, felt the long weapon buck in her hands and saw the surprise in the face of the man who had appeared, when the .44 lead whacked into his right thigh. It seemed that, concentrating on Conrad, he had failed completely to see the woman lying in the shallow trench. To Laura, the marvel was that she had not only managed to discharge the pistol but that she had actually hit what she had shot at. Conrad had turned as fast as he could, and as Walsh — for that was who he was — raised his pistol again, Conrad fired and hit him in the chest and sat him down. Walsh fell over sideways and lay twitching.

Incredulously, Laura said, 'I did

it . . . ! Bob, I did it! I hit him!'

He nodded, dropped to one knee, pressed a gloved hand on her back, making warm contact, but now heard another voice, Culpepper's, deeper than Jago's, call, 'Zac?' When he got no answer, he called, 'Arn?'

For the first time, Conrad raised his voice. 'They'll not hear you, Culpepper, if you go on hollering 'til Kingdom Come!' That beckoned another silence. It ran on for so long that Conrad began to wonder if at last they were about to try to rush him, taking their chances. Soon it became plain that, at any rate, they had believed him, about the dead men. A slight breeze was coming from the south-west, scarcely detectable though, where Conrad and Laura were. And from that south-west quarter, now, rose smoke which soon drifted over their heads, and they heard the gathering rush of fire among dry brush.

When Conrad saw Laura's involuntary movement, he said, 'Don't get up from there, you'll stand a better chance where you are.'

With the rushing of the crackling fire, the thin, whitish smoke was increasing, passing over them, casting urgently-moving shadows, dipping and lifting, sharp in their nostrils, stinging their eyes.

Bending closely over Laura, Conrad said, 'As soon as the worst of the fire's burned through in that direction, one patch to the next, they'll come walking in after it. The smoke will be blowing away from them. Likely they'll be in a line, strung out. Use the pistol. Fasten on one man. Shoot at him as often as you're able. Rest your elbows on either side of the trench so they'll take the pistol's weight.'

Conrad's tired, reddened eyes were streaming, and the acrid smoke was fiery in his nose and throat. Ducking away, he moved several yards to the right of where Laura lay, knelt down and pressed fresh loads into the slot, reloading the Winchester to its full capacity. Then he waited.

Still the smoke was coming over and the sound of the fire was fiercer now, and waves of heat were arriving, along with drifting black and white ash, some of which settled on them. The sandy clearing seemed very small now, as though it must soon be overpowered by the fire, brush burning now on either hand, some greener brush sending up clouds of thicker smoke which went boiling into the air, climbing swiftly and rolling as it went.

Laura, a gloved hand raised to her face, was peering between fingers, through narrowed, stinging eyes into the moving smoke, not wanting to miss the first glimpse of them. Her heart was pounding. The events of the coming minutes would mean survival or death, for she had made up her mind that, if Conrad was shot down she would stand up and advance towards Jago and his men, contriving to keep shooting at them until they were left no option but to kill her. And she was surprised that, having set her mind on that intent, she had been invaded by a strange calm, the like of which she had never before experienced. Fatalism, she supposed, a clearing away of all terrors, an acceptance of death, if that must be the outcome. She slipped a glance towards Conrad who was crouching a few yards from her, a dark blue bandanna now tied to cover his nose and mouth, hat pulled down. She raked around with one hand and grasped one of the canteens and in an awkward motion flung it towards him. He nodded, reached for it. The other canteen she unplugged with her teeth, tilted her head back and tipped some of the warmish water over her face, then rolled half over and took a long, mouth-slopping drink. Within a very short time she was in position again, holding the cocked pistol in both hands. She heard Conrad say, 'There . . . !'

Sure enough, through the smoke, she could distinguish some moving shapes.

Just as Conrad had predicted, they were following the path of the fire, walking in, spaced some yards apart, only shadowy figures as yet, of men who were perhaps not able to see Conrad clearly, or her at all. Laura fastened her whole attention on the one who, to her, was walking on the left of the line, a bigger man than the one in the middle. A bigger target. It would be difficult for her, but she desperately wanted to hold her fire until she had at least some chance of hitting him.

When momentarily an eddy of smoke sharpened the advancing shapes, she judged her chosen target to be about fifty feet from her, this man carrying a pistol; she gripped the Smith and Wesson and compelled herself to remain calm and focused. This time she was not startled by the jump of the pistol when she discharged it.

Conrad heard the Smith and Wesson go off but he was occupied in lining up the man directly in front of him, on the end of the line, and who now shot at

Conrad with a rifle, burning a fireline across Conrad's upper left arm even as Conrad let go a shot and hit the man squarely and bowled him over in the smoke-haze. Laura's pistol blasted again and the two men still standing, a very thin man and a much bigger one who clearly was hurt, went scurrying away. The skinny one had been Jago and even as he lost sight of him in swirling smoke, Conrad, his eyes hurting as though they too must be burning fired again but did not believe he had got a hit. It was all hard work now, for Conrad. He was very much aware of the pain just below his left shoulder and had to release a hand from the rifle. But he went across to Laura. 'You all right?'

'Yes . . . I'm sure I hit one of them . . . Bob, you've got blood on you.'

But Conrad went to ground in a hurry as lead came whipping in. Jago was by no means giving up. The smoke was much diminished now, a whole area of brush no more than blackened, smoking, skeletal branches. Conrad and Laura were exposed, now, to an attack from longer range. Laura wriggled down in her trench for there was nowhere else she could go. To stand up and run would almost certainly be fatal. Conrad, however, though he was now lying down, rifle ready, was in all likelihood quite visible to those bent on killing him. They had come in but had been compelled to retreat, one of them wounded. This one, Conrad thought, was Culpepper. They would begin shooting with precision. And around what was now the perimeter of their chosen place, three bodies lay smouldering, and the sickly-sweet smell of them could not be ignored.

A bullet kicked up sand only a yard from Conrad's face. Conrad shot at the place he thought the rifleman to be, and at a movement there, shot again. An arm was flung up and Conrad was quite sure that he had hit that one. No more firing came. Conrad waited. He did not know for how long he could hold up, his side paining him again, and the fiery poker across his upper left arm throbbing. He got to his knees, then struggled to his feet, dusty, dishevelled, bleeding. One way or another he had to finish this. He began going forward. He had got no more than five paces when he heard Laura scream 'Bob . . . !'

Like a man in a dream, Conrad turned. And there was Frank Jago, behind Conrad, coming through the smouldering brush that had been burned, pistol in hand, arm extended. Laura was struggling to bring the Smith and Wesson to bear, Conrad to raise the Winchester, and Jago, teeth bared, narrow chest heaving, like a man demented, came to a stop, yet curiously was failing to get the killing shot away. And suddenly, the pistol drifting off line, Jago with his rouge-like red cheeks and his sunken eyes, convulsing, head bending forward, vomiting gouts of bright blood, staggered, let go the pistol and fell to his knees. The noises coming from him were from the ravaged remains of his lungs as he heaved and rackingly coughed his life away onto the smouldering earth. The disease that had pursued him for so many years had come for him in its finality at the instant of his triumph, his moment of reckoning. If Ord Jago had reached from the grave for Dave Dryden, then maybe, some might say, Dave, or Ed Maidment, had now reached for Frank Jago.

Conrad sank to the ground. Laura came out of the trench and went to him. Neither she nor Conrad were aware of the horsemen until they heard a shout of command and looked up to see the lance-flying guidon of Lieutenant Bridges' smoke-misted detachment, having ridden to investigate a fire, coming to a halt forty yards out.

15

A porter had gone on ahead of them and they had now left the hotel, on foot, and were approaching the depot. Conrad, his face more gaunt than once it had been, but the face of a man who was in good health, was dressed in a grey broadcloth suit and a new, dark-grey townsman's hat. Laura, walking beside him, linked to him by one of her gloved hands, was wearing a mauve travelling cloak and a deep-purple tricorn hat.

'Rather you than me,' she was saying. 'In Daverne, years ago, I found Mr Poindexter of South-Western a cold individual. I couldn't take to him.'

'And I couldn't disagree,' said Conrad, 'but he does have one outstanding virtue, he's straight. An honest man, Poindexter. After all, it was he who saw to it that the consortium paid out for Frank, even at this late stage. An' for Culpepper an' Harries.'

'So you're quite sure he'll see to it that both the women are found and paid their shares?'

'I am.' A third of the accumulated bounties to Ruth Corde, a third to Eloise Dryden. Widows of the Conrad Posse. The only known next-of-kin. 'Oh, an' the cold Mr Poindexter asked me to offer his congratulations to the new Mrs Conrad.'

Laura had to smile.

Here was the depot. So the tall, darkly moustached man and the small, neat, very good-looking woman on his arm walked unhurriedly along the steamy platform to the standing train and he handed her into a car and stepped in after her, bending his head. A well-dressed couple. A man and his wife embarking on a journey.

RIDERS OF RIFLE RANGE
Wade Hamilton

Veterinarian Jeff Jones did not like open warfare — but it was there on Scrub Pine grass. When he diagnosed a sick bull on the Endicott ranch as having the contagious blackleg disease, he got involved in the warfare — whether he liked it or not!

BEAR PAW
Nevada Carter

Austin Dailey traded two cows to a pair of Indians for a bay horse, which subsequently disappeared. Tracks led to a secret hideout of fugitive Indians — and cattle thieves. Indians and stockmen co-operated against the rustlers. But it was Pale Woman who acted as interpreter between her people and the rangemen.

THE WEST WITCH
Lance Howard

Detective Quinton Hilcrest journeys west, seeking the Black Hood Bandits' lost fortune. Within hours of arriving in Hags Bend, he is fighting for his life, ensnared with a beautiful outcast the town claims is a witch! Can he save the young woman from the angry mob?

GUNS OF THE PONY EXPRESS
T. M. Dolan

Rich Zennor joined the Pony Express venture at the start, as second-in-command to tough Denning Hartman. But Zennor had the problems of Hartman believing that they had crossed trails in the past, and the fact that he was strongly attached to Hartman's Indian girl, Conchita.

BLACK JO OF THE PECOS
Jeff Blaine

Nobody knew where Black Josephine Callard came from or whither she returned. Deputy U.S. Marshal Frank Haggard would have to exercise all his cunning and ability to stay alive before he could defeat her highly successful gang and solve the mystery.

RIDE FOR YOUR LIFE
Johnny Mack Bride

They rode west, hoping for a new start. Then they met another broken-down casualty of war, and he had a plan that might deliver them from despair. But the only men who would attempt it would be the truly brave — or the desperate. They were both.

THE NIGHTHAWK
Charles Burnham

While John Baxter sat looking at the ruin that arsonists had made of his log house, a stranger rode into the yard. Baxter and Walt Showalter partnered up and re-built the house. But when it was dynamited, they struck back — and all hell broke loose.

MAVERICK PREACHER
M. Duggan

Clay Purnell was hopeful that his posting to Capra would be peaceable enough. However, on his very first day in town he rode into trouble. Although loath to use his .45, Clay found he had little choice — and his likeness to a notorious bank robber didn't help either!

SIXGUN SHOWDOWN
Art Flynn

After years as a lawman elsewhere, Dan Herrick returned to his old Arizona stamping ground to find that nesters were being driven from their homesteads by ruthless ranchers. Before putting away his gun once and for all, Dan forced a bloody and decisive showdown.

RIDE LIKE THE DEVIL!
Sam Gort

Ben Trunch arrived back on the Big T only to find that land-grabbing was in progress. He confronted Luke Fletcher, saloon-keeper and town boss, with what was happening, and was immediately forced to ride for his life. But he got the chance to put it all right in the end.